ROOM FOR LOVE

YEAR ONE BOOK SIX

MARGUERITE MARTIN GRAY

Always room for love!
Marguerite Gray '23

Becca, 11-8-23
I hope you
enjoy reading
my Mama's
novel.
—Katie Gray

ISBN: 978-1-951839-98-7

Celebrate Lit Publishing

304 S. Jones Blvd #754

Las Vegas, NV, 89107

http://www.celebratelitpublishing.com/

To my husband, Wayne.
Thank you for sharing the journey with me,
whether across the oceans,
to the mountains or the beaches
or in our own woods.
It's a sojourn I've enjoyed for all these years.
Where are we going next? I'm all in!

1

---

lexandre Island, August
The warm, cuddly bear hug from her only son would have to comfort Amy Lee through the next several months. As Joshua pushed away, Amy shivered, feeling dysfunctional and oddly alone. Closing her eyes, she envisioned a five-year-old little boy swinging and skipping between them—his father supporting him on one side and Amy on the other. The three of them dreamed of an adventure among the islands. Then the three become two and now…now with Joshua's inevitable departure…one.

"Mom, I'll be home at Christmas." He towered over her five-four stature, sharing the six-foot realm as his father had. His hands grasped her shoulders, forcing her upward gaze. "You promised me. No tears. Hmm?"

What a silly promise. She swiped at the corners of her unfaithful eyes. "Yes, right you are. Don't worry about me. Maison Cachée and my guests will keep me hopping." She glanced at his two friends, standing at security. "You will have the best time at university. You don't want to keep your friends waiting too long."

He pulled her to his side and kissed the top of her wind-blown hair. "I love you, Mom."

She managed a quick rise on her toes to plant one last kiss on his cheek. "*Au revoir. Vas-y!* Go have the time of your life."

As his boy-man form, dressed in non-island attire of blue jeans and a polo shirt, disappeared through the security booth at the Laumua airport, Amy's hand fluttered goodbye in front of her heart. Her promise to Neil was fulfilled after twelve years of rearing Joshua on her own. Well, handling on her own if she didn't count Maki and Luke Harmon. She had depended on them every day, even before Neil passed away.

Once outside the airport, turning toward the marina, Amy breathed in the fresh sea air and let out all the anxiety of letting her son disappear amid the laughter and backslapping cama-raderie of childhood friends. Hopefully, the University of Oregon would unmask the potential of the young men. The powers that be must have seen something or they would not have accepted them.

God, I'm alone, really alone. No Neil and now no Joshua. Now, I have...no one.

Forgive me. I'm never really alone, am I?

Her stride shortened and slowed. Her long flower-patterned skirt billowed around her ankles. The print and lightness of the fabric failed to brighten her outlook. Why race to the boat? When she got home, the house would seem empty, even with guests coming and going. If Maki guessed Amy's downtrodden thoughts, she'd redirect her to the plaque on the kitchen counter. "So be strong and courageous!" The rest of the passage Amy committed to memory. "Do not be afraid and do not panic before them. For the Lord your God will personally go ahead of you. He will never fail you nor abandon you."

As Amy stepped onto the boat, a memorable tug produced a playful grin. Maki walked a solid line and held to concrete beliefs when it came to God's Word. She had secured the verse almost immediately after Neil's death. "If you can't believe His Word, there's no use in displaying His Bible or singing His praises."

If she didn't want another lecture, Amy better claim the verse again. Somehow, God would help her conquer and progress in this new phase of her life. But no matter the words He used to comfort her, she still felt so very alone.

The small cabin cruiser had seen better days, but like a faithful friend, *Rosie* kept on performing her duties. Amy's husband had bought the boat fourteen years ago when they decided to try their hands with a bed and breakfast establishment. Amy used the boat to cart supplies from the islands and ferry to different meetings, friends, and shopping. A few times in the boat repair shop over the years returned *Rosie* close to new.

Amy stuffed her medium length hair under a straw hat, securing it under her chin. A glance in the side mirror reflected a tired green-eyed woman looking older than her years. Even the brown strands of hair escaping the hat strained to reveal health and vibrancy. Part of her shook and determined to say "This will not do. Something has to change," while the other more dominant side stoically held its ground. "You are tired and worn, and it doesn't matter."

A ten-mile jaunt to Alexandre Island on the boat released some of the tension, though niggling reminders twitched, wanting to surface and declare "all is not fine." She relished the time away from her normal duties, enjoying the fresh breeze. Yet, the duty of being a mother fit her and already left a void. What if they had been given more children? Why hadn't God given them others while there was time? What if...

To the wind and the sun, Amy shared, as if to a best friend, "What ifs never help. The past is over. I must embrace the now, today. For the first time ever, I can take care of me. I have to do it."

That didn't sound quite right, even as the thought drifted away across the waves. *Me? I don't even know who that is. Not really. Neil's wife. Joshua's mother. B & B owner. Church member. But me? It might be interesting to figure out.*

Amy never tired of the lush scenery—the same as she had discovered on her honeymoon. Jointly, they had fallen in love with the island culture, people, and laid-back island time and lifestyle. The cliffs on her right faced the islands, forming a circle, each connected with a similar history yet thriving on unique oddities as well as eccentric artists and local customs. The green cliffs fell to wide, sandy beaches, not rocky with black lava, as on other stretches throughout the archipelago.

Many boats dotted the horizon to her left. Familiar faces occupied the local vessels. Fourteen years tendered many occasions to float in and out of society's festivities and celebrations. She'd tasted the treats and shared the venues of each island, but always tethered her heart to Alexandre. Her home. Her heartbeat. Her life.

Maison Cachée hid among the flowering trees—a taste of the South Pacific with banana, coconut, papaya, guava, pineapple, and mango. Amy added the avenue from the dock to the house with alcoves, benches, and statues as a welcome for the guests, acclimating their senses. The walkway widened to accommodate a golf cart or small jeep for transporting goods or people. Most guests chose to take in their first view on foot, leaving the luggage for pickup.

After mooring the boat under its covered shelter, Amy grabbed her big straw bag, surprisingly light, for usually a trip to Laumua meant bags full of essentials. Today, she left her list at home and returned empty-handed. Saying goodbye was not easy and shopping would not have been a cure. Unlike her return home without Neil years ago, Amy's outlook on life and her heart bore different weights. She'd see and hold Joshua again. The difference rested in the strings, for she no longer had

4

a hold on him. On purpose, she cut them and permitted him to fly away, returning only when he wanted.

If he wanted. Her parents had relinquished their hold on her, and this was where she landed—thousands of miles from their home. And where was Joshua going? Back to Amy's roots a few miles from her parents. He had allies in the city, help in the wings. Would she be needed anymore?

I have You, Lord. Teach me again to let go and let You lead.

The hibiscus and bougainvillea, scattered among the other blooming shrubbery, bowed to her entrance from the path into a garden paradise, one cultivated with her own hands, guided with expert local gardeners. They were her therapy in the years since she'd lost so much of the will to remain and continue what she began as a partnership.

Even the word "partner" rang truer and stronger than "sole proprietor."

Picking a yellow and red hibiscus, she placed it behind her ear. A chorus of young voices chanting a local ditty about a dolphin and a sea turtle seeped around the corner. Quickly depositing her bag inside the door, Amy followed the melodic tune to the big log-sewn barn a few hundred feet behind the house. The children stood in a half-circle facing Maki and her niece, Nadine.

Amy wanted to jump, dance, clap, or all three at the sheer sound of joy but refrained out of fear they would stop at her absurdities—a thirty-eight-year-old woman jumping for joy at a simple tune! Instead, she sat in a bright red Adirondack chair, pushing her hands under her legs to curtail her enthusiasm. Her heart beat with the drum, handled by a small boy.

She had forgotten today was Monday. What else had she let slide into an abandoned corner, swept aside for another day? How many things had she labeled unimportant in her son's impending departure? Well, not her guests since her livelihood depended on their care. Not her son since her promise to prepare him for life and college or a job had ended (or been handed over.) Not the garden or the fruit trees since they branded La Maison Cachée. After all, without the beauty of the exotic grounds and promise of a tranquil stay, she would be breaking a trust with her American clientele.

She studied her answer. Somehow, they had been sequestered out of sight for a few weeks while Joshua had precedence. This passel of eager native Suamalian children. Her dream. Her inspired effort to bring an extra layer of education to the locals. Hope for the ones who could not hop from island to island to go to school or attend special seminars or classes. At one point her dream had been for a few children to come together after school for tutoring and extra help. Then the dream grew to a program called *Les Rêves*—Dreams. Amy desired for them to bring their dreams to the classroom.

Staring at the twenty bright-eyed students, Amy's heart leaped with purpose. Three years later, a converted barn welcomed future artisans. The log barn with a tin roof emphasized its age of the once-functioning plantation. As the oldest structure on the property, the French settlers had lived in the barn while the construction began on the main house. Although the outside appeared two hundred years old, the inside hosted four open classrooms separated by bamboo screens, and a large area for programs and gatherings.

The sharing of dreams echoed within the walls. *Les Rêves* hosted anywhere from five-year-olds, who wanted to be fishermen, to fifteen-year-olds, longing to pilot rescue planes or fly across the ocean.

Closing her eyes, she soared across the Pacific with her son. Joshua called their little school a "technical" one. But Amy, believing in big dreams, clung to the image of a place where dreams came true. Now, his place was an ocean away, a whole world removed from the log barn.

Clapping coerced Amy's attention to her surroundings.

6

Maki's lesson today focused on music. In the summer, the program for the children was three days a week for a few hours, alternating between crafts, music, and sports. Maki never failed to sprinkle hymns and praise songs among the native or French ones.

Turning to the audience consisting of a few guests and Amy, Maki bowed and waved her arm out to the side. The grins on the faces of the students of all sizes exploded with the applause.

Amy led with her whooping and jumping. *"Fantastique, mes amis! Très bien. Encore. Encore."*

The mini-concert ended with "He's Got the Whole World in His Hands."

Yes, He does. Thank you again, Lord. And please keep Joshua close.

Amy avoided any chance of commiserating with Maki or other staff and disappeared into her house. A cup of tea in hand, she curled in her oversized chair, overlooking the garden, and let the quietness and solitude envelope her.

ugust—New Mexico
Dr. Walker Standish stuffed his hands in his pockets and peered over his reading glasses. He overheard one of his students question if he had any other pants and jackets. Ignoring the comment, he chuckled. Yes, a closet full. He decided a few years back to stick to a less imposing choice factor. He could change the shirt and tie without messing with the coordination of the pants and jacket. His late wife had spoiled him by being his sounding board for life and his magical clothes wizard. His khaki pants and blue sports jacket served as his standard uniform as a professor of anthropology and archaeology at the University of New Mexico in Albuquerque.

Perusing his office on the third floor of the science building, Walker lamented the fact that she'd laugh at the way he packed up his office. He'd be back in six months but the maintenance and grounds crew would be updating and painting in his absence. His books, artifacts, and personal files and mementos had to be boxed and stored. Anything of worth he'd take to his house in the suburbs to gather dust. One of the closed rooms could act as custodian.

Reading glasses in his jacket, keys and phone in a pocket, boxes taped and labeled, Walker ran his fingers through his longer than usual thick hair.

I'm out of here. For now.

An earned and much needed sabbatical pushed him homeward. A journey he craved, other professors envied, and his daughters misunderstood. The grieving continued even after the girls had moved on with their lives. He was the only one who had remained as a cemented statue. Yet, they complained about him going on a wild, sojourn to the past, to an unknown South Pacific Island. Well, if they listened more and ranted less, they'd figure out the Suamalie Islands were very far from deserted or backwards. He compared them to Hawaii or Tahiti. Both girls shrugged and rolled their eyes, not in disrespect but in pity. Pity for their old Dad left to his own devices.

Forty-four was hardly too old to begin a new journey. Rebecca encouraged it. Discovering the treasures of these islands had been on his (and their) bucket list before the accident that had drained her last breath. It was no one's fault. A storm, a tree in the road, and a cliff. A driver's nightmare. And now his. If only he had been with her. Maybe he could have stopped or swerved—or not. Then the girls would be orphans.

Asking God why again would get him nowhere.

Peace, I leave with you. My peace I give you.

He claimed the verse in John, yet still his heart was troubled, and he feared the future. At least, his daughters had received most of their youth and impressionable years under their mother's brilliant tutelage.

Heaving a box of valuables into his arms, Walker exited his office—his university home for over ten years. He'd return in March to conduct seminars before the summer session when he resumed his teaching schedule. Why did this feel so permanent? He'd return to the familiar after this detour. He shook off the stray premonition, stored the box in the back seat, saluted the impressive brick campus building, and drove home.

3

*W*alker's hand barely touched the handle before it sprang open, as if on its own.

"Surprise!"

The "surprises" echoed off the walls and around the furniture from two dozen well-wishers. Well, he *hoped* they were bringing good wishes. Even his daughters bounced with glee at a *fait accompli*.

A girl on each side, he accepted their cheek kisses. "You got me. I don't understand, but I am surprised."

At twenty-four, Megan, the oldest by four years, probably concocted the scheme with Lucy agreeing to the opportunity to host a party. His five-eleven height reigned six inches above his girls, both the same height as Rebecca. Some of his favorite photographs were of the three standing with arms laced behind the others' backs, all so beautiful.

Megan leaned in, resting her head on his shoulder. "We wanted you to have a nice send-off. It's not every day the absent-minded professor ventures to worlds unknown."

"I'm not..." Oh, why try to explain? The absent-minded part had a history based on false accusations. The parts unknown tended to be a sore point since the girls refused to believe the Suamalie Islands even existed.

Lucy pulled down on his jacket. "Let's go meet your guests and dig into the food." Her hand found his as she pulled him into the melee of friends.

He recognized a few female colleagues who had tried unsuccessfully to introduce him to the dating game. Two years seemed too short a time. But so would ten years or twenty. The dating scene posed as a spider web full of sticky and poisonous scenarios. Was there such a thing as a nice, good spider? Rebecca had held no qualities of the arachnid. Yet, she was not here, nor it seemed any of her species.

I'm okay with that. One love in a lifetime is enough. If only I could convince the single women around here of that. Why can't they mimic the opinion of his daughter? The last thing they want is another female in the role of mother.

"Dad, snap out of it." Megan snapped her fingers, making him blink.

"Sorry." In her eyes, he always did something wrong. She marched to the other end of the table. Somehow, he would do his duty for his girls. Eat a plate of hors d'oeuvres, drink the punch, laugh, chat, while what he'd rather do entailed research, packing, and seclusion. No one understood. Nor did he. This innate desire to escape lingered because God designed it or Walker fueled it. Either way, he'd leave in two days.

He held up a sausage cheese ball. "This is really good. Did you make these, Lucy?" His youngest took after Rebecca in the kitchen. He chuckled at Megan, who avoided the recipe box, replacing her time with continuous debates and writing, both part of her teaching at a local public high school. Unlike Megan, Lucy was not one to verbalize her anger or disappointment. Walker didn't know for sure if she was as frustrated with him as her sister.

Lucy nodded before turning her brown eyes toward him.

Just like her mother's, big and soulful. "It's Mom's recipe."

Plopping the remainder in his mouth, he tasted the familiar spices, even after two years. "Perfection. You have her gift."

"Well, maybe that one. But I'm not creative like Megan and Mom."

"Maybe not in the same ways. But your desire to help others with creative ideas is something not all people can do. Your sociology degree will take you far."

Lucy shrugged. "Who knows? I might end up with you in some foreign country."

Megan rounded the table. "Not me. Albuquerque has all I need. You'll see that, Dad, after you stay a while on a deserted island."

Shaking his head at the repeated statement, Walker tried again to get his view across. "Do I need to sit down with you again, Megan, with a map and a tourist guide? I'll not be roughing it. I'm staying in a nice bed and breakfast, not a tent on a beach."

Crossing her arms, as he imagined her doing in front of her teenaged students, Megan positioned her stance for a lecture— he hoped short and low-key. A party wasn't the place for a loud reprimand from his adult daughter-turned-guardian. "But Dad, you don't even have permission to join the dig on the islands. What will you do for six months? Weave baskets?"

Not a bad suggestion. "I don't have to work in my field. I could sleep every day until noon, then lay on the beach and drink some kind of fruity mixture every day. Relaxing and reading on a sabbatical are enough. I'm reporting to no one." Though true, he planned to fill notebooks of research and read a shelf of books.

Her lower lip protruded in its predictable pout. "You could also stay home and do the same sort of thing. New Mexico has archeological digs that would welcome your expertise."

Hanging his head and clenching his jaw, Walker restrained

any words that could harm the evening. He cupped Megan's beautiful round chin with his fingers. "I'm going. And I'll be back to spend my dotage digging into New Mexico's past. Let me do this, please. We'll all be fine. I'm fine."

His stoic daughter let one wayward tear fall onto her finger. "All right. I'll say no more. Let's mingle a bit more."

He doubted her silence on the subject would last.

Walker departed on a day both girls worked or attended school. The taxi ride sealed his determination to confront his past and his loss and experience a positive future full of potential. He carried no grand expectations of a new career or change of address, but for six months he'd exist where the unknown could heal his heart and soul. Perhaps.

As he exited the cab, the summer heat engulfed him from above and below. One element he'd trade for a few months. Tropical climate might be enough of a change to cure his blues.

Red hills and gray deserts disappeared beneath him. Traveling attached naturally to his job. Archaeological digs with his students or as a visiting professor occurred every few years. His wife and daughters had accompanied him on several trips to Greece, Egypt, and Italy. This trip—vacation, reprieve—captured a different element of travel. Not sharing it with another person whom he knew promised an adventure unlike any he'd had before. The whole sabbatical thing could fail, and it wouldn't matter. He had nothing to prove. If he chose, he could have a silent retreat with a book a day.

Would he rather have Rebecca with him? Of course. Even the girls. But he believed God said go. Go alone. Hopefully, Walker didn't misinterpret the message.

This is where I'm supposed to be. In the air, chasing my destiny. Alone.

14

4

L a Maison Cachée

Stubborn weeds. With as much time as Amy spent pulling up the misguided plants, she remained surprised when one survived among the botanic bonanza of color. Her chronic urge to create an aesthetic garden entrance prohibited the hearty green vegetation to mature. Perhaps if she let those weeds be, she'd discover they had just as much beauty. After all, they had existed on the islands since the beginning.

Her discarded vegetation reached to the brim of her basket, defining a stopping point. A few more. Always more to pull. Surrounded by the citrus scented air mixed with gardenia, Amy thrived when her guests sought island pleasures around the grounds or beyond, or relaxed in the hammocks or coolness of their rooms. Breakfast cleared and replaced with fresh fruit, cookies, and nuts on the long table to stave off immediate hunger meant the afternoon was hers. Her time to accomplish chores—gardening, arranging flowers, inspecting rooms, or hiking on the mellow beach or the grassy slopes snaking into the mountain interior.

Today, she planned to stay close. Of the eight registered

guests, four arrived yesterday afternoon. First day guests always had questions about where to eat or to swim. Shopping and excursions topped the list of priorities. Who better to ask than the owner? Sometimes, brochures couldn't satisfy as well as the words of a local. Years ago, she achieved her tourism certification from the bureau in Laumua. The perks included all the latest news on events, programs, businesses, and ideas—both local and for each island. It was a no-brainer to keep the certification updated.

One more guest, scheduled to arrive this afternoon, had booked a suite for six months. She couldn't think of a better way to spend half a year. Or in her case, half a lifetime.

Nadine ran the front desk in the afternoons, leaving her time to work on online classes in the morning. The nineteen-year-old took advantage of her native status, receiving several scholarships from a French university in Tahiti. Amy would hate to lose her one day, but wanted the best for the golden-toned beauty with ebony hair. If she stopped studying economics, she could become a model. Amy had wondered why Joshua and Nadine never dated. Of course, dating his "sister" explained the reason. They'd grown up side by side for fourteen years.

Oh, to be young and have your whole life ahead of you.

Amy's straw hat protected her from the sun hanging in the ludicrously blue sky. The gentle sway of the palm trees and the cool breeze prevented sweat from invading her afternoon. Nothing pressing beckoned her inside. Nadine would handle the new arrival.

Pushing herself up from her kneeling position among the jasmine and lavender, she thumped her hat securely on her head before stretching toward the heavens. Her right hand bumped a solid mass. Quickly bringing her hand to cover her mouth in surprise, she eyed a tall stranger on the path. Only the guests used the paths and grounds.

"Excuse me." His American accent extinguished all concern. Without a doubt, he was the newest guest. "I don't mean to bother you. I thought I'd admire the gardens, then you popped up unexpectedly."

Amy shaded her eyes with her hand, blocking the sun and bringing him into focus. "No need to apologize. I'm just glad you didn't get covered in weeds or hit in the face. I must remember to glance around before I stand."

Dropping her hand, she continued her study from beneath her extra-wide brim hat. He was a good half a foot taller than she was. Dark hair, more the length of an islander than a continental dweller. Brown eyes—tired and curious. Khaki pants and a blue blazer. Those would have to go. She couldn't leave off the smile, one that touched his eyes, removing a bit of the wear and tear.

Shaking off her detailed perusal, she remembered her role. "May I help you?"

"I don't know. I'm getting acquainted with the grounds. And as the gardener, you'd know better than anyone what I need to see."

The gardener? Well, she'd been mistaken for a housekeeper, a painter, a mechanic, and a cook. A gardener appealed to her. Perhaps she could do it full time.

She giggled at the moniker. "I would be happy to point out some of the highlights of the grounds." No need to spoil her fun. They'd be introduced soon enough. "This way." Her discarded weeds would make it to the compost later.

He followed her to the end of the sprawling house. Six of the twelve rooms faced the front and six the back. His rooms were at the end, containing a sitting room and kitchenette within the suite. But as the gardener, she wouldn't know that. Surely, Nadine had shown him his dwelling, or should Amy say "home." She hoped he'd feel that way for such a long stay.

He let her do all the talking, although she gave him ample

opportunity to ask questions and comment. The silent type. Either full of confidence or lacking it. He didn't carry himself like someone out to prove himself, to gain a position in society, or obtain a promotion. If he wanted quiet, he came to the right place.

Rounding the corner by his rooms, they surveyed the full extent of the luscious landscape from a gazebo tucked among spreading jacarandas to a lawn edged with every hue of hibiscus to a pool, hosting electric blue depths to a crystal waterfall cascading from the jade jungles.

She breathed in the blended scents of the earthy wilderness of the surrounding forest and the sharp aromas of the exotic flowering plants. "This is one of Maison Cachée's secrets. An oasis, offering the best of island life."

The handsome alien spoke as if forced by nature. "An oasis among many south sea idylls. It feels like another world."

"It is. You might leave it, but it never leaves you. My advice is to let it transform you." She winked at him. "It will, you know."

She left him standing at the edge of the marvelous view. Being mesmerized deserved a bit of privacy. Retrieving her basket, Amy disappeared to change into her next role as hostess for the social hour before everyone dispersed for their evening meals on the island.

Walker recognized the views from his suite as the same ones the gardener—*I wish I knew her name*—had shown him. He had the best rooms in the house. The old plantation dwelling had the appearance and feel of an island home. Far from the plantation houses in the United States. No giant columns supporting two to three story white mansions with rooms the size of whole apartments under fifteen-foot ceilings.

This place, elevated on thick solid blocks, had a central

entrance, opening into a spacious living area large enough to seat thirty people. Walker guessed the area to the right contained the living quarters of the owner, perhaps half the size of the area for the guests. The thatched huts by the log barn could be dwellings for the staff.

What a brilliant idea! I wish I'd thought of it. Turning an old plantation into a rambling bed and breakfast, highly efficient and a productive business.

Would he be able to meet the owner? The historic features of the house and land didn't stray far from the subject of archaeology. He rubbed his hands together, liking the idea of exploring the area. Why not begin here?

Walker debated over what to wear. His wardrobe choice included the black jeans Megan forced into his suitcase and a pair of khakis. It might be cool tonight, so his standard blue jacket would suffice. He could change it up another day. Perhaps buying some local attire. In the mirror he checked his long wavy hair, realizing he should have cut it before his departure. His clean-shaven face felt good after the long flight. He wouldn't promise the same look every day. If he went into absent-minded archaeological mode, he'd forgo a daily shave. But the hair? He'd never resort to a pony tail. Or would he?

Following the voices and beat of drums, Walker strode the length of the hallway with hands in his pockets. He knew no one. He'd never had trouble making friends, but did he want one? Here he didn't have to divulge any information at all. His choice. What did anyone need to know about him?

Browsing the small crowd, he noted the casual atmosphere. Shorts and untucked shirts. Jeans and T-shirts. Colorful skirts and flip-flops. Walker glanced at his brown lace-up leather shoes, tucked-in shirts, and pressed khakis. He chuckled. He might need some help. His daughters, thousands of miles away, would chide him—again—on his choice of clothing.

He grabbed an orange fruity drink from a tray. Smelling the

mango scent, he had a quick sip, enjoying his choice. At least this one contained only fruit and sugar. Maybe social hour was better than cocktail hour.

A man with a flower-printed shirt joined Walker. "I'm Thomas and this is my wife, Ruth."

"Nice to meet you. I'm Walker. How long have you been here?"

"Only a few days. We're from Southern California, checking out the islands. Our friends gave this place raving reviews."

Small talk was always Rebecca's forte. Walter nodded a lot. "I read about these islands and the archaeological digs. I'm hoping to join one."

Walker watched the other groups. One lady in an orange, flowing skirt with a white over-sized blouse flitted from guest to guest. Her short brown hair, pinned back at the side, rested on her shoulders. She, too, held an orange drink. Would she make her way to his group? A hostess of sorts? Or the owner? Most likely.

With a fluid pivot, she faced him. Her grin reached her eyes as she raised her glass to him. The gardener. His cheeks heated and twitched with embarrassment. From gardener to owner in a few hours. She definitely had the advantage. After speaking to Thomas and Ruth, she turned to him.

"*Talofa*. Dr. Standish, I presume." She raised her glass to him.

Their glasses clinked as they laughed. "You knew all along. How *un*hostess-like of you. You must be Mrs. Lee."

"Why, yes, sir, I am. But please, I'm Amy to all my guests. It might take you a while to adjust, but formalities are a bit loose here."

Her green eyes sparked as the light reflected off the crystal glass. Playful. Carefree. Yet searching.

"Walker. No doctor or Standish, please. I can gladly play this island game."

"Oh, it's not a game, Walker. It's real. Whatever agenda you are used to in—what state?"

"New Mexico." A world away.

"Right...in New Mexico. That agenda will not work here. Don't get me wrong. You're among the educated, wealthy, and world-traveled here, but step away a few yards and the real island mystic begins. Enjoy your stay."

Poof. She sailed away in an orange puff.

5

_____

*C*hiding herself for her swift, early exit last night, Amy chalked it up to too much sun. Liar. She had no more sun than usual. It was those velvet brown eyes. No, his sheepish grin, as if he knew her secrets. What secrets? There were very few secrets on the islands. And those buried in her heart promised to remain unearthed.

She had shocked him. The proof wrapped around his dropped jaw as she twirled away. Who pivoted and twirled at her age? She refused to call it flirting. Never, ever, flirt with the guests. He could be married, since it wasn't a question on the registration.

Sitting in her office beside the front desk, Amy had a new calendar, her notebook, sticky notes, and colored markers ready for mapping out the new school year. In two weeks *Les Rêves* would open again as an after-school program for tutoring and extracurricular activities. The schedule included ten volunteers, mostly from the local village church. God placed caring believers in Amy's path to share in the dream of *Les Rêves*. Oh, how she wanted to expand to include more music, art, cooking, and another language, and eventually reach out to other islands.

But that proposal would take more than her calendar and paper. She'd need a ream for that and a large bank draft.

For now, her eight and a half by fourteen papers taped to her wall would have to do. *A plan is a plan. As a promise is a promise.* She'd given her word to over forty potential students, and she'd see it through.

Blue for five-year-olds. Red for…

Knock, knock. Why now?

Capping her marker, she peered through her reading glasses, forgetting she couldn't see far with them on. The whole bad eyesight thing was new to her. She tossed them aside.

"I'm sorry to disturb you, Mrs.…Amy. No one is at the desk."

Her smile, genuine enough, relinquished her frustration about the school. "Have a seat, please. How may I help you, Walker?"

His well-built, not-a-pudgy-part body slipped into the comfy loveseat. "First, the breakfast was superb. I don't think I can eat that well every morning for six months without running it off daily."

"That is one use of the beaches. In a few steps you have nature's track. Better than a football field." Did he even like sports? He'd not find the teams he was used to here.

He grinned. "Thanks for the suggestion." He glanced at her unorganized desk.

What must he think? How could one run a successful business with this mess? "I'm not normally this…well…this chaotic. I have a project I'm coordinating." Vague enough?

"I see. I'm not so immune to the task of organization like data and schedules if you need any help."

She ran her hand over her papers with no chance of covering the mess. "Thank you. I'll keep you in mind. You might earn your keep over the months if you have a hankering for volunteer work." *Hankering? Use your words, Amy!*

Walker rested his chin on his fist and widened his smile.

"Well, what I really need is a local guide. Do you know of anyone? I want to explore the island and don't know where to begin."

Amy leaned back into her chair away from her project, exchanging it for another dilemma. *This one is different. He's serious about his search.* "I suppose you're not searching for the normal tourist excursions or you would have found something within the myriad of brochures."

His frown pinched his cheeks. "I browsed through them. I'm sure I'll find a few of interest. I hope I didn't offend you."

"Oh, not at all. Be assured, I only support and put out the brochures for the activities I personally trust and approve."

His smile returned. "Yes, I'm sure of that. But you are correct. I want to steer away from the crowds and get a feel for the island. This may sound strange." He lowered his voice and leaned forward. "I want to connect to the heart of the past through the present."

Not a psychic, crystal ball type, I hope. "As in a mystical way with seances and local hexes?" Her skepticism escaped, though if he truly felt that way she'd apologize and leave him to his own entertainment.

His guffaw calmed her heart rate a tad. Although he could be using it as a cover of the truth of her words. "No, Amy. I'm not a mystic trying to talk to the dead. I'm an archaeologist. Part of my role is to understand the history and people of an area, before I try to piece together a past from the rubble."

That is so much better. The rumble started deep in her chest and exploded with a snort, a grunt, and a roaring laugh. Both hands covered her mouth. Dare she say anything? Her voice squeaked. "I'm so sorry. I'm not laughing at you. I pictured you in Suamalian costume, dancing to the old chants in order to summon an old native chief. I do understand, and I'd love to help you."

Elbows resting on the arms of the chair and chin on top of his hands, Walker searched for her sincerity, or something else from the recesses of his gorgeous eyes. He sure had seen a few of her bad characteristics—dirty hands and wild imagination.

She did want to help him. "If you can trust me, I'll introduce you to Kato, Nadine's friend. He has a tourism certification just as I do, which means he can be hired to be your guide."

His brows lifted. "As you can too?"

"Well, yes, except I wouldn't take your money. I might go along just for the fun of it."

"I'd like that. Of course, when you have the time." He pointed to her disheveled papers.

"Yes. This will be organized within two weeks since that is when the after-school program begins."

He leaned forward. "Tell me more about this school. I'm a professor. Education is my livelihood and my passion."

"Oh." *More qualified than I am.* "The doctor must be for education, not medical."

"Precisely. I could not set a finger or a leg."

Fifteen minutes later, Amy had another volunteer, and Walker had an occasional tour guide. A firm handshake sealed their deal.

Amy walked him to the foyer. "I anticipate good things from this partnership, Walker."

"Not nearly as much as I do. All aspects meet my purpose for this sabbatical."

All aspects? Did she fit in there in any role, other than guide and hostess? No, she knew her boundaries. Dr. New Mexico resided on his own island with a deep lagoon and high cliffs. Both of which Amy could never cross.

In his ideas about how he'd spend his time, helping with an after-school program with a beautiful entrepreneur hadn't entered his realm. But the prospect of relating with native islanders charged his anthropology battery. Perhaps this arena would divulge some interesting data. Of course, Amy would not value his research using her program as a data-driven research endeavor. He'd have to dwell on that aspect. The last thing he planned to do was disrupt her community school.

Before he firmed up his involvement with the tutoring, he intended to gather information about Alexandre Island from the perspective of a local. He had Kato's information on his temporary "Office" desk. The spotty Wi-Fi supposedly worked best in the morning. After turning on his laptop, he searched "Kato—Local Alexandre Guide"—not very original. But why would he need a branding and marketing scheme? The young man would have plenty of business, especially with Amy and Nadine vouching for him.

"Approaches to the island untainted by tourists. Swim in a sea cave. Kayak to a forgotten beach. Walk on a suspension bridge. Explore hyper-colored reefs. Visit ancient sites and burial caves. Climb on huge volcanic rocks. Snorkel around a shipwreck. All on island time. Suggestions welcome."

Hmm. Ancient sites and shipwrecks—an archeologist's paradise. Walker procured his notes about the island. On the southeastern portion, an archeological dig started and faded with rumors of reopening. The association had his name and number. If he could gain access to the site with a local who had ties, he might have a chance of participating at some level. Perhaps Kato or Amy knew the owner. It appeared to be tribal land, earmarked for preservation.

Jumping ahead would skip some major steps. Foremost, Walker needed to walk to the village—Belle Vue, was it?—for food. Breakfast could only take him so far. The suite had a kitchenette, but most of his meals would be eaten elsewhere. He could have tagged along with other guests. But a venture on his own appealed to the whole point of the sabbatical. He had no one—not one soul—to care for except himself. Megan and Lucy would not appear at his door with meals or steal away his quiet evening. His colleagues wouldn't drag him to another social, making sure his grief hadn't consumed him. No lesson plans or staff meetings.

He had six months of meetings of one. Could it get more selfish than that?

A professional journey or a personal escape? It didn't matter. Walker was here in paradise. He had the choice to make it anything he wanted.

Right now, his stomach hinted at finding an island café on the beach with a breeze and a fruity drink, with or without an umbrella.

Taking the trail through the forest—or jungle—tickled his senses with the mingled fragrances of the flowering trees and the vibrant, bold hues of the canopy above him. He refused to carry his pocket guide of flora and fauna because then he'd stop every few feet and look up the name of every plant. No, once he had a guide, he'd bombard him with questions.

The wide, well-worn path emptied onto a graveled street lined with huts. Not expecting any cars, Walker walked as others did in the road. Curious about each shop and dwelling, he knew he had months to explore and only a few minutes to conquer his hunger. The road curved and continued along the beach.

Laughter drew Walker to a long open structure with a coconut-prong thatched roof. Tables with colorful umbrellas set on the beach. His stomach gave him the clue that in the Fête Hatch resided relief. *Bring on the hearty fare.*

A tall, lanky mid-thirties waiter in cut-off shorts and a restaurant T-shirt set a glass of water and a basket of something interesting on the table.

With a chuckle, the waiter commented, "*Talofa*. You are new here, right?" Perfect English. How did he know? "Those are coconut crisps—fried to perfection."

"*Fa'afetai*. Thank you." Walker stared at the trifold menu. "I could study this all day. What do you suggest for an island newcomer who is anxious to try it all? I'll be here for six months, so just start me off with your favorite."

The young man, "Tony" on his pin, pointed to the pictures. "If you want a taste of Suamalie, I would choose crab Rangoon for an appetizer with the macadamia hummus, mahi mahi with clam sauce, rice wrapped in banana leaves, and Samoan *panikeke* for dessert."

Walker's belly crescendoed at the choices. "I'll take everything but the dessert for now plus your house specialty frozen drink without the spirits."

"That would be Belle Pina—a pineapple concoction."

If it was anywhere near the explosion of flavor of last night's drink, he'd be willing to try any new flavor.

He looked out to the sea. Each view surpassed the last. Surely, after a while his senses would settle as normalcy set in. Or would he constantly be on high alert, anticipating the scene around the corner? The villages positioned on the east side of the island had the sunset behind the mountains. He'd have to catch a sundown another time, maybe a boat ride around the northern coast for an evening on the western sands. For now, the sun's rays lighted up paths across the ripples as the waves hit the shore. Pink, purple, orange ribbons. He'd have to wake up early for a sunrise, many sunrises.

The cool pineapple perfection lulled him into a sweet coma of idyllic schemes. He knew better than to permit his days to flit away like the waves without accomplishing anything. He'd allowed his routine of teaching and planning to meld into a monotonous pattern—perhaps at first, one for healing. If he could cocoon himself in the ordinary and familiar, he could survive and hang on to his former life. Yet, after two years, his former life never materialized. It left the day Rebecca passed away. As much as his daughters clung to the sameness of the traditions, it wasn't the same. It never would be. He chose a reprieve. So far, he considered his choice the right one. What could go wrong with an island, the sun, and the people?

He had no plans to make lasting friendships. He had some of those at home. Anyway, the more people he cared about, the more losses he would face. This adventure would be his alone. Study the culture and the people without attachments. A history research project. A benefit to all. He'd leave a record for the citizens and a paper in a journal. An album of personal photographs and a volume of notes to add to his files.

Nowhere would he find a broken heart or promises. Only deep personal relationships developed scars and pain. Books, paper, artifacts, and ancient sites held no power over his present. He would be safe.

And most of all he had God's promise. "I am with you wherever you go."

Used to eating alone, Walker surmised the rabbling in his head was company he'd keep—no strings attached. The savory cuisine buoyed him for the night until the breakfast fare tempted his taste buds again. Rubbing his belly, he committed to runs on the beach and hikes in the forest to keep the inches from creeping up. Six months in paradise, eating his fill of island specialties with exotic spices and tantalizing mixtures, would be full of temptations. The saving footnote rested in the amount of seafood and fruit included in the dishes.

The route "home" followed the beach to the pier. He turned toward the east and witnessed the sun reflecting off the distant waters, offering a technicolor sunset for other islanders across the sea. Turning west, his back to the water, he blinked, adjusting to the bright orange and red filtering through the tall palm and coconut trees.

Have I thanked You today, Lord? You provided this retreat. Now, I want to be a worthy recipient.

6

*W*ith sandals swinging in her hand, Amy progressed along the beach as her toes dug into the wet, warm sand. The day had been long, but the checkmarks by completed tasks earned her a stroll in the dark. Her guests and tourists tended to keep to the left of the pier, giving them easy access to lighted paths, hammocks, and entrance to the grounds. Amy chose the less traveled shore with a rugged vista of huge island rock formations and dense forests and rugged cliffs.

When her nightly ventures became a permanent mode to quiet her restless, lonely spirit, Maki convinced Amy that a few solar lights along the tree lines would not take away from the ambience. They would push back the darkness and curtail any wandering night life.

The stars hung low tonight. Either that or her heavy heart needed the extra heavenly bodies to work their magic.

Joshua had rung earlier. "All is fine. I love everything about college life."

"Even the food?"

"Yes, Mom. I'm glad you warned me about the easy access of

sweets, especially ice cream. I run every morning so I can eat my share."

She sighed. "I miss you." She missed everything about him. Preparing his meals, doing his laundry, helping with his homework, sharing in the chores. Swimming and walking with him on the beach. Co-existing in their home.

When did her house become so big and empty? She couldn't fill the space except with silence.

Her toes curled around a round shell. An abandoned crab shell or inhabited. Either way, she threw it back.

Out in the open with the gentle waves from the sea calling with the night calls of forest birds and distant drum beats from local abodes, Amy prayed often. God touched these islands centuries ago with the missionaries bringing the truth of Christ. Before that, He created the beauty, forming the Suamalie Islands into a ring of gardens of Eden delights. Perfection as only He could perform. She acknowledged His hand as she tried her hand at gardening. How could she embellish perfection?

With the undulation of the ocean as her guide, she lifted up her gaze, spread out her arms, and added her prayers. "I know there's no reason for me to tell You what is going on in my life. But here I am releasing my praise for Your blessings and Your provision." She sighed. "Thank You. Forgive my weakness as I complain about missing Joshua. I feel some of the same anxiety as I did when Neil left. I wander the house, seeing Joshua in everything. I try to read but I can't. I fix meals but don't eat much. TV offers little companionship. I had no idea I depended on Joshua to give me meaning. It's like Neil leaving all over again."

Yet, Joshua is alive and well. I just need to listen to Your guidance and fulfill the purpose You have for me, no matter how long it takes.

God was always right. It was not as if she remained truly alone. Of course, she had God's presence all the time. Maki and

Luke, Nadine and Kato, all the children, her guests, and she still had Joshua, just not in the same house.

Her hands fell to her hips. *I can do this, and do it with contentment. I may not be happy all the time, but I can learn to be content in my current situation.*

Pivoting for the walk home, Amy caught sight of an elongated shadow close to the pier. Someone braved the darker, secluded beach as she did. The shadow moved then halted. Advancing, she noted a man in khaki pants and a blue shirt. He carried his shoes in his hand.

Walker. One of the many who graced her life, rendering her not alone though still lonely.

"Walker, I see you found your way home from the restaurant."

His strides brought him into the water beside her. Their footprints washed away with the ebb and flow. He turned toward the sea. She imagined newness attacked all his senses. It did that to Amy often when she allowed the awesomeness to penetrate her realm.

His voice, low against the constant moan of the waves, soothed away her blues. "As wonderful as my suite is, I couldn't give up this view quite yet." His gaze locked with hers. "Do you ever tire of this?" His hands reached to encompass the starlight reaching to the earth and casting ribbons of light across the vastness.

She shook her head and turned her body toward the sea. Perhaps, if she saw her surroundings and her life with new eyes and expectations, her woes would dissipate. "No, I never tire of it. But I do think I underappreciate what I have before me at a mere glance."

His head drooped as if studying his wet pants legs and bare feet. "All too soon the familiar can disappear."

She knew that too well. Twelve years and it seemed so raw,

festering at a mild memory or word. Not knowing his story, she could only guess at his reference.

The silence lingered, not bothering her. Two strangers on the beach, enjoying the beauty and the effects. They didn't owe each other an explanation, not this soon. Over the next six months, they might share but not necessarily.

Clearing his throat, he lifted his head and drew his left hand forward. The stars twinkled, bouncing their light off a solid gold band. Married.

"I lost my wife two years ago. A car wreck. She disappeared with no time to prepare."

Oh, so recent. She touched her ring finger where she once wore her wedding band but not for the past five years. Walker had a way to go if Amy's grief was the norm.

Whispering into the breeze and the warm night air, Amy added, "Even with time to prepare, it's not enough."

"You lost your husband?" She nodded. "I didn't know."

"It was a long time ago. Twelve years." Or was it yesterday? Depending on the day, it could have been recent. *I'm not going to tell him that. He has to deal with his own grief, in his own time. Who am I to offer advice? I haven't exactly moved on, at least not very far.*

She searched for words as she tilted her head, probing his face for answers or encouragement. Maybe he didn't need her comments or empathy, but God nudged her forward. "I cling to this verse from John's gospel in the Bible. 'Peace, I leave with you; My peace I give you. I do not give to you as the world gives...'"

His deep, soothing tone finished with "Do not let your hearts be troubled and do not be afraid."

"Yes, that's it." She threw her head back, and from someplace deep, laughter bubbled and met his as he joined her. Pure release.

The laughter pierced the night air, leaving both with broad

grins. She halted the stillness with backward steps. "Who would have thought a verse about peace would lead to laughter."

They walked side by side toward the pier. The solar tiki lights lined the path to the house. How her heart could be any lighter she didn't know. The stars. The water. The stranger. And the laughter. A remedy for the doldrums.

The next morning, Walker found the feast of a breakfast with a renewed vow to minimize his lunch, if he had any at all. At nine o'clock he joined the breakfast crowd. How many guests would he meet over six months? He didn't know how Amy remembered all the names, but she did as she added delicious concoctions to the sideboard.

Today, he tried gooey pastries with apricot preserves and French toast with blueberries, always hoping the pancakes from the first morning would rotate into the menu soon. He wrote in a notebook what he ate because he knew his girls would ask, making sure he ate healthy items and a lot.

He had admitted his lack of appetite and weight loss once to them and never heard the end of it. They were mother hens, Megan more than Lucy. In the past year, he had worked out in the gym and eaten his fruits and vegetables like a good child. His form appeared in better shape than before his life changed so drastically. It felt good and right to have strong biceps and quads again.

Running on the beach would help him maintain his structure. Maybe a dig or two or some manual jobs to help around the house would build his upper strength.

Thomas, the Californian, occupied the seat next to Walker. Leaning in, the man whispered as if he had a grand secret. "You must buy some island clothes. The attire isn't very different from California. But you guys in New Mexico must not own a pair of shorts." The man chuckled, clearly trusting his opinion mattered.

Surprisingly, it did matter. The man's input stirred Walker to seek help from Amy. After all, she'd know best where he could purchase a more appropriate, casual wardrobe. He almost laughed at himself over breakfast. What a dull picture of a boring professor. Under his breath he promised to ditch the khakis until he returned to the mainland.

Watching Amy disappear into what he assumed was the kitchen, Walker followed, hoping to gain her input. He liked her hair pulled back with a big red scarf that matched her wide-legged pants. He credited the flower apron for how she kept her white T-shirt clean.

"Excuse me, Amy. Could I ask you a question?"

She set the dishes in a large copper sink. "Of course. How may I help you?" Was the twinkle in her eyes from their shared laughter on the beach? The first of many memories over the months ahead.

He stuffed his hands in the familiar pockets of his old faithful khakis. The ones he bought over and over. Six pairs now? "I think I need some island clothing, and I don't know where to start."

Her hand covered her mouth but not the giggles. "I see. I think I can help with that." Her grin crinkled her eyes, a unique green like a shade of island vegetation.

"Great. 'Cause I think Tom will call me out every day until I find some."

"I'm taking the jeep to the market in Nouvelle Lorient a few miles from here. It would give you an opportunity to see a bit of the island and to shop, although the main island of Laumua has more of a variety."

Shop. He hated the word. His daughters had volunteered to be his personal shoppers but his needs were met with very little variety. Until now. He hoped Amy would have pity on him—no flowered shirts or big island logos like the tourists. He wanted to dress like Kato and Luke, not Thomas, although Thomas appeared more Walker's age.

When did he achieve middle age? A place where he resided, neither young nor old. It should be the prime of his life. Perhaps this sabbatical could be labeled a mid-life crisis. Instead of a red convertible, he chose a tropical island.

Laughter and music traveled through the foyer from the back veranda. "If you care for a drink, we have a very creative barista. Raymond's specialties are non-alcoholic smoothies. I chose a long time ago to leave the heavy stuff to the resorts and restaurants."

Walker gravitated toward the carefree cadences of people enjoying each other. Were they truly without cares or just knew how to relax in the moment? "Would you join me?" He gestured with his hand toward a spare table.

"I have...that is, I must..." Her hesitation surprised him. Was he being too friendly with his host? He certainly didn't mean to cause any anxiety. "Yes, I will. My paperwork can wait."

He almost sputtered a silly reply in relief. That was all it was. She had work that resulted in indecisiveness. "What will you have?"

"Coconut, mango, and lime with paprika."

His crinkled nose and wide eyes reacted in uncertainty. "You *do* know that doesn't sound very consumable, right?"

"Oh, but it is. Try it." Her green gaze, filtered through long lashes, offered a challenge.

Shuddering while curtailing an audible "yuck," he smacked his lips, strode to the bar, and ordered not one but two frozen coconut, mango, lime, paprika drinks. Raymond's smile and wink in Amy's direction convinced Walker that he wasn't the first guest to fall under her cocktail spell.

The view of the estate from the porch, though entirely different from the riveting waves and starlight patterns on the beach, held as much exotic beauty. He sank into the turquoise cushions, resting his heel on one knee. Amy melded into her chair, relaxed with her head resting on the back cushion, eyes closed. That pose must come with time. He feared he'd miss an island jewel, whether a bird or a breeze. Amy inhaled the island, and the island breathed in her liveliness. One needed the other.

He didn't feel that way about anyone or anything.

Walker checked the screen before answering the call. Megan. He pulled in an extra helping of air, letting it prepare him for the lecture. She meant well. He preferred her role of daughter over the one of caregiver or parent.

"Hey, Dad. How are you? I hope I'm not calling too early."

He faked a yawn. "No, not at all."

Giggling, she mimicked him, except hers sounded real. "It's late here. I just needed to hear your voice."

"How are you and Lucy?"

"Nothing new—school for her and teaching for me. The same old stuff, while for you I can't say that."

"You are right. I have a new favorite drink—coconut, mango, lime with paprika."

"Ugh. Surely, you can find something else. You must be starving."

He laughed as he thought about the breakfast feast in an hour. "Hardly. I'll send you pictures of the fish and vegetable dishes I've had so far."

She sighed. He knew that came with shaking her head and pursing her lips. "Don't you want to come home, Dad?"

"What? After three days? No way. I'm here for the long haul. I've not even started exploring. There are caves and burial grounds and digs and..."

"I know. Old stuff waiting for you to unearth. I get it, kind of. You know I worry about you. Who is taking care of you?"

Oh, Megan. Your heart is big but misguided right now. Wisdom, Lord. I need some.

"My darling girl. I'm capable of taking care of myself. I'm even going shopping today for more appropriate island clothes."

"That's scary. Surely, someone is going with you. I can't imagine the result if left solely up to you."

Chuckling, he knew she had a valid point in her criticism. "I asked the proprietor to guide me to a reputable shop. If it makes you feel better, I'll send you pictures of your new dad."

"Without khakis, a polo, and a jacket? I can't quite visualize it." She paused and clicked her tongue. "It's all right if you want to come home. No one will think any less of you for trying without completing the six months."

"Megan, that's not happening. Please drop that line of thinking." *My adventure has barely begun, dear child.*

Probably pouting as only Megan can, she continued her all-knowing speech. "You always told us to honor our commitments. Remember when I begged to sign up for ballet classes, and you and Mom said 'fine' as long as I saw it through the year."

They had a battle then. "I do. By Christmas you wanted to quit, and we said no."

"Well, you can quit if you want, Dad."

Would this be a weekly battle? Walker hoped she'd find another angle, or better still, stop the worrying and parenting. "Right now, I need to go eat the mouth-watering breakfast. We'll talk soon. I love you, and give Lucy my love."

"Bye, Dad. Love you too."

Am I ready for this adventure? Could Megan be correct in her prediction that I need to go home? To the familiar. To the memories. To the same old schedule that fits me perfectly.

At eleven o'clock, Amy drummed her fingers on the steering wheel of her ten-year-old jeep. She'd stick with paid-in-full items such as her house and vehicle over the monthly notes. Watching her nest egg grow gave her confidence in her investments. A solid growth portfolio bode well for her retirement, not that she could conjure up that scenario anytime soon.

Checking her watch again, she positioned her body toward the foyer, straining to see if Walker was wandering around aimlessly. Island time must agree with him. Usually, she accepted the laidback timeless atmosphere, but today she had things to accomplish.

Where is he?

"I'm right here." Walker stuck his head through the passenger window.

Did she say that out loud? Probably, since a mischievous grin revealed his pearly whites more than necessary.

She patted the seat. "Well, let's go."

He used the roof of the jeep to guide his body and khaki-clad legs onto the seat. For a second, she felt his brown gaze ask questions, which was ridiculous. What would he want to know about her that he didn't already know?

His comfort in her presence radiated through his casual pose, elbow on the window ledge, his long, rich, dark curls flowing in the breeze, and his other arm draped over the seat.

He's a guest. It's not as if I've not seen a man recently. Although he is very handsome and sure of himself. Surely, we can be friends. That's it. Friends.

Her new friend let his eyes roam the scenery. "Where are we going first?"

Amy ran her fingers through a few strands of carefree hair at her neck, a habit of wrapping them around her fingers before releasing the curls. "Le Bon Homme. The least touristy men's clothing shop in Nouvelle Lorient. I'll let you loose in there while I go for school supplies."

His head jerked sideways. "What? You're not going with me?"

A quick glance saw wide eyes laced with a tiny ounce of fear, as if seeing a spider or insect creeping close. "Do you need my help?" Remembering his khakis and polos, she guessed he did.

"Oh, yes. Please. I might come out with more of the same." He gestured to his attire, then winked at her, replacing his fear with laughter.

"All right. You might have to return the favor by helping me organize an excursion."

Now why did she do that? She'd completed all the details. She'd analyze her out of the ordinary musings later. He knitted his brows. Just what she needed, two confused individuals. He bowed as a knight doing her bidding. "At your service."

"It's in a few days on Tiga. The festival always proves to have something for everyone." She searched the public parking lot at the edge of town. A handful of spaces remained. "You might want to cancel your volunteer service."

"Why?"

"Oh, I think I'll give you the role of herding the guests."

Her quiet giggles rocked her shoulders. Someone aiding her in the roundups sounded marvelous. Joshua had tried his best but always found someone his own age at the events, being no help at all.

"I've been here often with Joshua, although he preferred going with his friends to the mall in Laumua." The same proprietor greeted her years ago with Neil by her side. All she needed to do was hand Walker over to the owner, Mr. Long.

A dark-skinned older man with white hair met them at the door. "Welcome to Le Bon Homme, Madame."

Amy leaned in for a hug. Fourteen years erased her shyness and formality. Although not a true born and bred islander, she'd

earned her place in this society. "I've brought a new customer."
For the man's ears only, she added, "He needs help."

Mr. Long extended his hand. "I'm Ken Long."

"Walker Standish." He threw Amy a quick smile. "I've been
told by a few unnamed people that my jackets and khakis will
not do."

"Ah ha. I think I have some ideas. I assume since Madame
has brought you here that the tourist look is not for you."

Walker ducked his head, appearing guilty and apologetic.
"My daughters call me the 'absent-minded professor.' And now
that I think about it, I've never seen one sitting on the beach or
resting in a hammock." At least he could laugh at himself.

Amy found a round chair hanging by ropes. She sank into
the black cushion. The swing motion could lull her to sleep. But
didn't she have a purpose? Not really. Walker and Mr. Long
would do just fine. Swing and relax? Or mark something off her
list?

"What do you think, Amy?"

She focused on her friend in navy shorts resting an inch
above his knees and a loose-fitting buttoned shirt in a washed-
out lighter blue. He even had a pair of brown sandals, probably
made of the durable leather-like rubber, good for beach walking
and the water. She forced her grin to remain neutral as she
noticed his pale legs and feet. The sun would color them soon
enough.

Her clapping caused the swing to twirl, adding drama to the
mix. "Perfect. It is a start. And you did it without a flower."

Walker held up a green shirt with a faded flower print,
barely apparent. "I *do* like this one."

"I think we'll make an islander of you yet. Subtle is good.
Now, multiply your outfits, add some pants and a light sports
jacket, and bathing trunks, if you don't have one."

Saluting her, he said, "Yes, ma'am."

"Be sure to add a festive shirt for the festival, perhaps in red."

He smirked. "Then can we find something to eat?" His eyes mimicked a child begging for a cookie or pleading for a treat.

Her jaw dropped, feigning shock. "What? Was breakfast not enough for you?"

"It sustained me through this ordeal." He turned to Mr. Long. "No, offense."

The owner had spent his time collecting a stack of shorts, shirts, and pants. "None taken. In a few more minutes, you can be on your way."

Amy settled deeper into the swing and closed her eyes. One successful errand accomplished.

Walker stashed his new wardrobe in the Jeep before joining Amy, waiting in the village. His long gait deposited him within a few minutes by her side. "How about some fish tacos? My treat."

"Follow me. There is a beachfront hut. We can grab a few and lounge under an umbrella."

He had taken Amy's suggestion and traded his pants for shorts in the store. Studying his legs as he walked, he supposed a little time in the sun wouldn't hurt. Wouldn't his daughters be shocked at his thoughts and his attire? Should he send a picture?

Minutes later, they found a table with an umbrella. Amy held a menu without studying it. "Franco serves the best sauce with his mahimahi tacos. It's sweet, yet savory, made with guava and coconut cream."

"I'm noticing coconut is used for so many dishes. I don't even notice the taste, as in a coconut cake or pie."

"It's used here like milk or cream. Since it is so abundant, every part has a purpose."

He laughed as he took his tacos in a coconut bowl to the lounge chair. "What did you order for me to drink today?"

"A sparkling pineapple soda."

"With or without coconut?"

After removing her sunglasses, Amy's green eyes sparkled with mirth. "You'll be begging to take home coconut everything when you leave."

When I leave! What if I want to stay? Silly, after only three days. I'll be missing my New Mexico cuisine and desert surroundings by then.

Amy stretched out her legs and settled her bowl of tacos in her lap. Today, she wore a denim skirt, exposing her well-shaped calves and knees. Her green shirt, a shade darker than her eyes, billowed in the breeze, showing off her muscular arms. *Casual yet elegant. Is that a thing?*

Wiping sauce off her chin, Amy caught him staring at her. He instantly reverted his stare to his drink. The last opinion he wanted her to have of him was one of interest. The whole *island* atmosphere messed with his priorities and long-standing goals.

"Eat up, professor. We have errands to complete. *Vite. Vite!*"

"*Oui, oui, madame.* By the way, this is my new favorite meal. Who knew?"

Empty bowls filled the tiny circular table between their chairs. She rubbed her hands together, swung her legs around, and stood. "Before long, you'll have a long list of favorites and a recipe book of ideas."

A recipe book for me to remember my once laidback life on a faraway island. Recipes for one.

7

*I*f Amy had a gavel, she'd use it to start the meeting, more as a lark than serious. A gavel in an old log barn with a large round table surrounded by eight people dressed in shorts and simple dresses didn't fit the motif.

Yet, she was serious about the after-school program. If her dream ever reached its potential, she'd need everyone on board, plus more money and teachers. *Les Rêves* had places to go if they managed to keep the momentum and excitement steered in the right direction.

"Welcome to our first planning session before our program for the children begins. I'll let you introduce yourselves to Dr. Walker Standish. Tell him what your role is and anything you want that will help him catch the vision."

Walker leaned forward, letting his posture relate the same message as his eye contact. He was no stranger to faculty meetings and planning sessions, but on a much grander scale. What a difference—an after-school program compared to a college program. His enthusiasm seemed to be genuine, at least with his questions and concerns. The project had its critics from the natives and the other citizens. But never from the child partici-pating. Where Walker placed his opinion remained to be seen.

Amy began with a brief sketch of *Les Rêves*. "We began our endeavor two years ago with five local children who needed a way to cultivate their skills and interests. Some came for tutoring in English, French, and math. Others found an outlet for art and music." She nodded at Maki and Luke, acknowl-edging their support from the beginning. "My role is to provide avenues for our young artists. I try to guide them to explore with the colors and subject matter. Some of my art hangs in this barn along with the students' work." She noted Walker surveying the walls where landscapes hung, some framed, some not. Each one of hers contained one bright spot of color—a ball, the sun, a flower, a skirt, a bird—that popped out on a calming scene—an ocean, beach, porch, café, jungle clearing, sunrise, or sunset. She didn't draw people, not yet.

Amy motioned to Maki on her right. "Next."

Maki waved. "I teach culinary skills and basic home economics and hygiene. Some of my students want to be chefs or nurses but most desire to help at home. We have a basic *non*electric cook stove for familiar use and the modern kitchen for more experience, giving them a chance to move into the villages or cities."

So basic, yet such a needed skill. Many of the children would never leave their clan or villages. But some reached out to explore a new way of life or to have an adventure.

Luke shared about his woodworking and mechanic skills. "The boys, and some girls, produce fine products that they can carry home."

Amy nodded to Nadine. "You're next."

"*Merci*. I have a few guitars, an electric keyboard, and drums. The children interested in music have melodic voices ready to share with their families and beyond. We put on a program at the end of the term. So, this one will be before Christmas."

What did this group look like to an outsider? Her personal involvement eliminated that view point. Her pride in her team sprung from her acknowledgement that God in His wisdom created the dream and brought it to fruition. Well, He was still blessing it since *Les Rêves* continued to grow and change. How would everyone feel about Walker's role? She wasn't quite certain it would work. She and Kato saw his purpose, but the others?

Focus, Amy.

She straightened and felt eyes upon her. "Sorry. I was thinking about the children singing carols in a few months. So, next. Kato, our star athlete."

The young man bowed his head at her introduction. "Hardly. But I appreciate your faith in my ability."

Raising his hand, Luke added, facing Walker across the table. "You'll learn that Kato has a few titles from his time at the big island high school. Trophies and ribbons in football—soccer to Americans—track, and baseball."

Kato's broad smile proved his acceptance of the accolades. "All in the past, Luke. But I do feel I have a few tidbits to offer the children. As a tribal native, I want to show them that they can succeed even outside of their present environment. I'll be offering skills to build teamwork as well as strengthen their bodies and minds."

"*Merci*, Kato." Amy's son had spent hours watching and trying to copy Kato's control over a soccer ball. They remained good friends, even though Joshua never became an athlete with Kato's skills.

Next to Kato sat Pastor Logan Turner, a man about the same age as Walker, in his early forties. He and his wife brought their two sons and daughter to the after-school program as helpers, but also hoping for friendships and acceptance among the natives. "Now, for our tutoring duo. Pastor Logan, would you please share your role?"

He reached his hand toward Walker and greeted him with a handshake. "Welcome to Alexandre Island."

Walker grinned, giving his total attention to Logan, as he had for everyone else. She knew he had a deep respect for God and His Word, but as for a close relationship with God she had not noticed. Another good reason to add Walker to the team. So many grew in their faith when connected with Logan and the local congregation.

Moving his head to meet all eyes, Walker's confident command in the group seeped through his voice. "Thank you. I'm impressed so far with everything I've heard. I do hope I can help in some capacity."

Logan laughed. "I'm sure Amy already has that mapped out. Saying no will be the hard part."

Walker turned toward her and winked. The blush creeping across her cheeks was not appropriate. She chalked it up to surprise, for no one of the male persuasion had winked at her for over a decade. Had Neil ever winked? Surely, he had. Why couldn't she remember?

Logan's words penetrated her heated detour. "I am available to tutor in math and science, although I lean heavily on the science manual for the intricate formulas and detailed experiments. Math comes a lot easier."

His wife elbowed him. "That is why he balances the accounts, not me." She chuckled and continued, "I'm Isabelle. Once upon a time, I dreamed of writing a bestselling novel, but I've found my niche with short stories and articles. I help the children with their English and French homework. A few have expressed an interest in the creative side."

Walker drummed his fingers on the table before facing Isabelle. "Have you thought about publishing their stories or poems? I'm sure a university would jump on that project."

Murmuring and sparks of excitement dominoed around the table. Isabelle nodded to each comment. Would she accept the challenge, the idea from a stranger? Amy had a notion he'd not remain an outsider for long. His six months might just be the flame they needed, igniting the fire for the future of *Les Rêves*.

Watching Isabelle's eyes glisten with tears, Amy put her friend's silence and emotions into words. The children tended to bring out strong sentiments. Amy may not have Isabelle's elegant words but at least had something to fill the void. "I think that is an excellent idea, Walker. Reading the team's expressions and hearing their chatter, I think that is a valuable option for our students."

Logan covered Isabelle's hand with his and patted it. Amy was confident it wasn't the first or last time Isabelle would let her tears speak volumes.

"So, now, Dr. Standish, let's hear from you."

He nodded without a wink this time. "I can lend my time in the area of history in general. But I have some ideas that might motivate the students to dig deeper and apply their knowledge. What if as a project, we concentrate on their history? Each interested student can showcase and research a part of their history. It could be clothing, food, rituals, battles, colonization, religion—anything to bring to light their connection with the past. This would be a safe place to do that, assuming the public schools don't already have that option."

The members shook their heads or shrugged. Kato and Nadine locked their gaze on Walker. Kato spoke, using his unique position as a native and a graduate of a national school. "I was never asked to share about my history. I tried to hide it so I would fit in with the European heritage group. This might give pride in their—my—history."

"Yes, exactly. Also, the older ones could be included in an archaeological dig if I can find one, unless there is a site here." His light brown eyes secured her stare.

"Kato and I have wondered. We'll share our findings with you on that." She laced her fingers together and studied them on

49

the table in front of her. So many ideas and dreams. Raising her head, she searched the eyes of each of the seven people gracing the table in the old barn. Counting herself, eight individuals trying to improve the lives of a few eager students. *Beautiful.*

"Before we start the scheduling, would it be all right to pray? More than anything, we need this to be God's purpose for the children. Our dreams without God's dreams are bound to fail."

As far as she knew every head bowed. Her confidence wavered, especially with Pastor Logan available. But the urge to pray aloud was greater than her fear or awkwardness.

"Father God, we are Your humble servants, hands and feet and words, to do the work of Your Kingdom even on this tiny island in the Pacific. You know our hearts—selfish at times—but greatly dependent on Your guidance and strength. We can't do this alone. We don't want to do it without you. Set all pride and gain aside, except that which glorifies You always. In Jesus' name. Amen."

Amens echoed around the table. Pulling in a deep breath, she pushed it out. The heady, spirit-filled atmosphere buoyed her for the rest of the meeting.

A low cloud cover hovered over the bay where a medium-sized party boat, at least that was Walker's description, moored at the side of the pier. As Amy's side-kick for the festival excursion, Walker followed her through the garden, down the path to the water. Her yellow blouse led the way, shuffling in the breeze, billowing toward him occasionally.

Head and eyes away from her mesmerizing form. I'm here to help with the guests, not study the hostess.

In two hours, the journey to Tiga would begin. Amy offered an early introduction to the captain and the boat.

"*Talofa,* Jean. *Nous sommes ici,*" Amy shouted. A tall, thin but muscular man with a trimmed beard ducked from the front cabin of the vessel. His wide smile matched Amy's. Walker envied the easy rapport she had with just about everyone. How long had it taken her? More than six months for sure.

I can't be jealous of what I can't have. Anyway, I have friends and colleagues at home. Home—four thousand miles away. A foreign land. A few days ago, Alexandre was foreign. When did my thinking flip?

The twenty-something-year-old stuck his hand out to Walker. "Jean Girard, *mon plaisir*, Dr. Standish."

"*S'il te plait, appelles-moi*, Walker."

"*Bien*, Walker. What do you want to see?"

Walker shrugged. "I'm mostly along for the ride. I know nothing about boats, so anything you share is a bonus and new to me."

Jean offered Amy his shoulder as she stepped onto the boat. Walker could play that role with the ladies.

The young man had a perfect grasp of the English language with a slight French accent. "The guests will be able to sit under the canopy or out in the open at the sides and rear. There are life jackets in the benches and up front behind the cabin. Water and cold drinks are in the cold chest. Restrooms are in the rear down the steps. The reminder of the lower level is sleeping quarters for myself, crew, and guests for longer journeys."

Walker perused the boat from side to side. "You have a nice set-up here. What do you call her?"

"*Suzette*, after my daughter."

"Ah, I'd have a problem then with two daughters. The *Megan-Lucy* doesn't sound quite right. How old is your Suzette?"

"Suzie is soon to be eight."

A young father like I was. Rebecca couldn't wait to start a family, so at twenty-two Megan had arrived. "Any other children?"

Jean dropped his head, and when he returned his gaze, Walker noticed the cloudy eyes as if the sky had suddenly darkened. He recognized the pain. "I'm sorry. I overstepped with my curiosity."

"No, it's fine. My wife left Suzette with me when the child was two. She ran to he States, away from the confines of the islands, escaping the only life she'd ever known. So, no other children nor another wife. No more entanglements for me. *L'amour* is for more fortunate men than I."

Moi aussi. One for a lifetime.

"Well, I hope you find someone. You are young. Who knows?" *And I am old—a big difference in perspective.*

Jean recovered from the foray into the past and strode toward the cabin. "Let's have a quick lesson at the controls."

"I hope you aren't counting on me to steer us out of any place."

"Ah, who knows, *mon ami?*"

Walker waited by the boat on the pier. His white shorts and green shirt, a definite improvement for his wardrobe, gave him a clean yet casual appeal. He comfortably embodied his role as greeter and gatherer.

Amy half swiveled her head to the side, seeing her brood of chicks waddling behind her, chirping away about the excursion, their plumage varying in degree of tourist attire. Sometimes, her hostess and tourist guide position made her giggle, for so often it was the same as a mother and her children. *Two by two. Hold hands. Don't push or run. Hurry up. Wear this. Be quiet.*

In her bag, she carried a red and orange striped flag on a stick to hold high when a group followed her in a crowd. Today, she had Walker where his job as rear guard would round up the stragglers—she hoped. It could be she asked too much of a paying guest. Joshua, of course, had joined her on these excursions without complaining. How many festivals and tours had he attended since age six or seven?

Hands in his pockets, leaning casually on the post, Amy could envision a seasoned sailor in a few months—tan and laid back taking his time. His smile reached his eyes, producing wisdom creases—she wished that for herself instead of age lines or wrinkles.

Pivoting to the group of ten passengers, Amy clapped to get their attention. "Before you board and scatter, there are a few instructions. Life jackets are in the chests. Please note the ones closest to you as well as the life preservers. The boat will not go fast or very far. We want you to enjoy your trip but be safe. If you need help onto the boat, Walker is here to help you."

She turned toward him, placing her hand on his shoulder, and stepped onto the deck. His hand rested on her back, as precaution in steadying her. The pressure released long ago sensations of walking on the beach with her husband, their arms wrapped around each other. Oh, this was far from an embrace, so why the memory? She received hugs from her friends all the time.

As if sparks might fly, she raced to the far side and concentrated on the crystalline, velvety blue-green sea. Deep breaths of the salty sea air cleared her disturbing thoughts. She had a role of guide for the afternoon, so whatever a guide persona entailed, she would do it. Smile, listen, and guide.

The couples scattered, some outside, some under the canopy, chattering the whole while. The newness of the experience took some time to simmer. Amu still viewed the sparkle of island life, leaving her in awe.

Jean eased the boat away from the dock, heading south to Tiga.

Walker advanced beside her. "May I bring you a drink?" His southwest accent resonated as familiar and soothing.

"Yes, water would be perfect." Her curious gaze followed his steps to the chest. What made someone escape to a remote island alone? He could have gone with a colleague or his daughters for a few weeks. But six months? Joining her husband was one thing, but alone? She wouldn't have done it. But here he was, doing the unthinkable.

She joined him on a bench that faced the view of the islands on the starboard. Jean always liked to give the tourists a glimpse of the other islands instead of progressing directly to the destination.

"I hope you have a chance to visit and explore all the islands. We're passing St. Alyn Island now." Amy pointed to the green land mass with its mountainous peaks. "Next is the Isle of Tiga. Each has its own unique offerings, though the lifestyles and basic attractions are the same. Agriculture and farming exist as well as plantations and orchards."

"Why did you choose Alexandre Island?"

She giggled. "I could ask you the same question. You had seven islands to choose from, and you chose Alexandre."

"True. But I'm not staying forever."

The hues of the water reflected in his blue eyes, mixing shadows and light. Better to peer into the sea than his curious depths.

She sighed. "We weren't planning on staying. It was a vacation. We chose Alexandre, as many do, for its proximity to Laumua, the airport, and modern conveniences. But from the first day La Maison Cachée felt like home. The owners wanted to sell, and we wanted to stay." A flood of memories washed over her as if all of it happened yesterday.

He wouldn't release her gaze. "It sounds like a dream."

As well as a true love story. Crossing her arms, she turned her body toward his, desiring to share this moment with him, an unlikely recipient of her rare confidence. Walker locked his focus on her. "A dream was hardly the word, for we never had mentioned owning a B & B before or living on an island. I guess we were young and invincible, naïve enough to think it would work. Four thousand miles from home was a bit drastic, but God had His own ideas for us. The owners turned it over to our care a few years before Neil died. I learned enough to carry on what had become our dream."

"Well, La Maison Cachée is beautiful. I chose it and the island for many reasons. From research, I knew the accommodations would meet my needs for a long stay. Since it is situated on an island with ongoing archeological digs, I felt I could do some research too." He let his focus drift to the island view before landing on her again. "After almost a week, I feel at home. The potential here is great."

She bit her bottom lip, concentrating on his response. He saw the island in a different light, expecting to uncover the past, and she'd revolved around the present. She'd never been on a dig, although she'd seen sites around the island. There were places on her property believed to be former dwellings. No one had questioned her about the caves or the mounds. Should she be interested or curious? Other land owners opened their private property to controlled, professional groups. Should she? Would it interrupt the peace she found?

At least she could contribute to Walker's experience. "Let's talk to Kato tomorrow about setting you up with a local archeological site. I'd like to see what is involved. Maybe it's time I stuck my hands and feet in the past."

His cheeks rose with his enthusiasm. "I'd like that. No, I'd love the chance." He patted her shoulder. "And even more if you come with us."

The thirty-minute trip ended far too quickly for Amy. Dreams and possibilities were colliding, morphing into something unexpected and dangerous. Could dangerous be a catalyst for change?

8

The rhythmic beat of the pate log drums and slit drums lured the tourists as if under a spell—an ancient code pulled from the solid rock of the island, letting loose through the souls of the drummers. Walker could not have remained on board even if he wanted, for the *tom, tom, tom* of the drums motioned him forward. Had anyone else felt the pull?

He acted as the rear guard, herding the guests. Their chatter could not overpower the cadence filtering from the hut on a knoll bordering the beach. Imagining the constant beat in his head as a permanent sound, he shook himself from the trance. The islands were hypnotic enough without the extra layer.

Amy raised her red and orange flag, and as obedient children or students, the group gathered around. He did a quick count—twelve. How many times would Amy try to count her chicks today?

"The hut behind me, Fia Fia Cove, is where we will gather for the festivities tonight beginning at six. It is buffet style with all the island favorites. For the next few hours there will be many events including canoe races, a beauty pageant, dance lessons, concerts, arts and crafts, food, and a flower show. Enjoy yourselves. I'll be around to answer questions."

Thomas stepped toward Walker. "Would you like to walk with us? I have a feeling my wife is going to disappear into the melee of shops."

He shook his head with a chuckle. *"Non, merci.* I'll enjoy wandering by myself. I'll end up people watching."

Joining his wife, Thomas headed away from the beach. Canoe races or a beach café? A museum would be nice. Walker set his steps toward the village.

A flash of yellow converged in his periphery. A welcome intrusion on his planning.

"Hey, Walker." Amy's hand squeezed his upper arm, bringing him to a stop. "Do you need some company?"

He shrugged. "Sure. Sometimes it's nice to share experiences. Where are you headed?" He rubbed his chin and pointed his finger at her. "You might be just the person I need. I know this will sound a bit boring to you, but…do you know if there is a local museum?"

She cocked her head and covered her mouth—or halted her laughter. Her eyes offered him surprise not ridicule. "I do. It's small but might have exactly what we want."

"We?"

"Why, yes. I spend time with the history and artifacts in order to understand the culture."

"Mrs. Lee, you surprise me. Not many people would choose a display of pottery over a shopping opportunity."

She bumped her elbow into his ribs. "Who's to say I won't do both?"

"Touché. You join me at the museum, and I'll roam the shops with you."

Sunglasses pulled back on her head with her hair bouncing on her shoulders, Amy radiated youthfulness and contentment with her life. It couldn't have been easy rearing her son alone.

"You have a deal." Amy grabbed for his hand but pulled back before he could latch on to her. "Oops, sorry. I'm used to dragging children or my son into compliance."

"No problem. Let's go." Preferably without the awkwardness of holding hands. His palms itched from tingles of a time in the past when holding hands was a daily reward after he returned home from work. His girls had now grown out of the act. No one had held his hand in over two years. He scratched his palm, relieving the negative train of thought.

"I'll put on my tour guide cap for a moment. The museum is housed in an old house dating to the French colonists around 1760. After a government initiative to preserve landmarks, it made the cut. The artifacts are from this island alone."

Walker clasped his hands behind his back and matched her shorter stride. "Does every island have a museum?"

"Yes. I'm sorry I didn't share that fact with you sooner. It's in the brochure about the island. Our museum is by the post office in Porte d'Or."

"I'll have to go there next week. There is so much to learn. I'm ready to get my hands dirty—literally."

The entrance fee was a donation box unlike the high dollar tickets in the states. Hopefully, his few bills would help keep the small museum open. A docent handed him a pamphlet with numbers and descriptions in French and English. Amy stuck hers in her bag. It would probably end up on her brochure table in the foyer of her house for the guests.

He studied the floor plan. "I like the way it progresses in chronological order."

"Me too. If someone doesn't like pottery then furniture and costumes for that era are mixed in. There's something for everyone, even children." Amy crossed her arms and leaned close to the glass. The display contained a 1700s room with a table and chairs, chimney, cooking pots over a fake fire, a cradle, a lantern, and a bed with a quilt.

While she stared, he tried to figure out her interest. His fascination rested with the pottery pieces and the furniture. Hers landed elsewhere.

She pointed to a side table. "Look at these books." She read the placard in front of each book. *"La Bible, Les voyages nobles,* and *Le journal de Marc Hebert.* They must have been valuable possessions from their homeland. Do you think they are copies?"

He clicked his tongue. "I would hope so. Unless this place has high security. Usually, books are treated as jewelry. But, now that I look closer, this glass seems to be thief proof."

"Which would you read first if allowed?" Amy drummed her fingers on her chin. "I'd choose the Bible to see all the names listed. You?"

"The journal. The daily life of the people inspires my work."

Amy walked on, shedding light on the progression of time ending with the late 1800s when the islands became a French protectorate.

Walker glanced around the last room after seeing the exit sign. "Where are the antiquities? The French weren't the first to occupy these islands."

"Ah. The archeologist emerges. Anything that ancient is on Laumua in the national museum. Not as large as the Smithsonian or the British Museum, of course, but just as grand and important. Anything four thousand years old deserves the best final resting place available."

Was she a secret archeologist? Or a closet historian? Maybe an absent-minded professor? "Well said. The museums and libraries of Laumua are on my list."

As they exited the house museum, a booming fog horn pierced the air. Amy clapped her hands and skipped forward, following the crowd. Swinging her head towards him, her green eyes sparkled. "The canoe races are beginning. You'll enjoy them. Brains and brawn working together. Who knows? You might develop a passion for canoeing."

Her skip became a fast-paced walk, one he easily joined. He'd take his cue from Amy's enthusiasm, living in the moment.

Fia Fia Cove offered the festival event to tourists during September in order to pull in money and their share of the tourist finances. Amy knew that her guests, and really any traveler to the remote islands, had money to spend. The locals benefited as well as businesses like hers. As long as the islands and her people were not abused and taken advantage of, Amy accepted the motives behind the events.

Amy had lost Walker in the crowds as he wandered the shops perusing the trinkets he could buy for his daughters. After releasing her feet from her sandals, Amy slowly traversed the sandy cove, letting the granules exfoliate more than her skin. The heat and slight abrasive activity eased her tension—all emotional and mental. Physically, she looked and felt fine, no complaints. Her emotions could use a thorough recalculation or reset. She'd aligned her life in the care of her son. Now, what would take his place and level her psyche? She could always find another project, but busyness, as she knew from experience, would not give her permanent stability. The adjustment must attach to her inner being, her spiritual connection to life.

Peace, I leave with you.

Peace, not busyness. Contentment, not perfection.

This wasn't the first time she faced change. At least, she knew she'd see her son again. Joshua needed his own life. There was no guarantee he'd return home to live.

I left my family. Why shouldn't he? If only the loneliness would lift. My work doesn't fill the rooms of my home or the rooms of my heart. I have so much love to give. There's room for love, but Neil and Joshua are so far away.

The constant beat of the log drums drew her closer to Fia Fia Cove and her agenda—count her chicks and guide them to their seats for the evening.

As she maneuvered the wooden steps, she noticed Walker corralling their group, taking his job as assistant seriously. She smiled, wrapping her mind around the idea of a helpmate, even if just for the evening with a bunch of tourists.

Holding the rail, Amy replaced her sandals then dusted off her sandy hands. "Thank you, Walker. Who are we missing?" She counted eleven including herself.

Thomas raised his hand. "My wife. She is lagging behind because she took her packages to the boat." Several laughed, probably since they had done the same thing.

"Well, that is a good thing." Amy knew the cathartic effect some received from shopping. She had tried that therapy, but it never conquered her pain or grief—not for long. "Our table is over here. We have seats in the center next to the stage—the first six on each side."

Long tables pushed together at the ends held twenty people on each side. The six rows offered various views of the stage, all spectacular, but Amy always tried to appease her small groups with preferential viewing. Personally, she'd rather the seats farther away for easy exit and less noise.

She stretched out her arm. "You are welcome to claim your seats." Hurried steps raced to the reserved end as if someone else would steal them. Always the same, until one was no longer a tourist.

Walker held back with Amy, chuckling calmly with only wiggling shoulders giving him away.

"I hope you are not making fun of me, Walker."

His hands shot up, palms out even with his ears in surrender. "Oh, not at all. I'm amazed at the scurrying motion of everyone.

It's the tourist effect. I tried to let the eager ones alight before taking my turn. It reminds me of college graduation ceremonies. Parents and family members rush to reserve seats hours before the event."

Grinning, she soaked up the same amazement. "It's human nature, I guess. We think we each deserve the best, whether a seat or food or a view." Stifling her own giggle, she added, "That reminds me. Don't let the other guests know about your suite. There might be a stampede at the front desk for better accommodations."

Leaning in closer, his height providing a canopy from the sun, he whispered, "My lips are sealed. I'm not giving up my rooms. I'll fight for them."

"Hmmm. That would be a sight to see but bad for business."

The queue at the buffet line formed quickly. Walker touched her shoulder, angling her in that direction. "While the others are claiming their seats, why don't we attach our priority to the food?"

She rubbed her hands together and licked her lips. "A wonderful choice. Food over seating every time."

He guided her with slight pressure on her back. Was it an unconscious gesture? Familiarity of a friend? Surely, the heat from his palm seared from her imagination, not actual warmth. Her nerve endings lacked any recent memory, having hibernated for a decade. A few years ago, she had followed the advice of a friend and attempted a few dates. Two was the most with two different men. Nope, dating at her age proved uninviting. Human touch, at least from a man like Walker— not family or a close friend—stirred distant sensations. Not good and not bad. But any stirring of emotion could not end well.

Amy picked up a plate. "I'll go first, so I can describe the food."

Walker followed her example, lifting a turquoise plate from

the stack. "I'll lean on your advice. I'll be a copycat until I know my own preferences. I'm not scared."

"Eel? Octopus? Squid? Sea urchins? Seaweed?" She raised her eyebrows. Some things she avoided—eel was one of them. Many continentals, especially land huggers, avoided other seafood delicacies. She'd see how brave Walker would be. "This should be fun."

Amy knew from experience that her plate would not hold all of the samples. "Polynesian cheese ball with pineapple, scallion, coconut, and macadamia nuts, luau ribs with peach sauce, beef satay skewers with tenderloin."

Walker added each so far. "Is it okay if I come back?"

"As many times as you like, but remember there is a boat ride back."

Seafood stuffed mushrooms, chicken *pupus*, salmon *poke*, meatballs, Teriyaki beef or chicken, fish tacos, pork and rice, *shoyu* chicken, eggplant in coconut cream, green beans, spiced cauliflower, dumplings with sweet coconut sauce.

Amy's taste buds somersaulted as a hill of food covered her plate. "We'll return for desserts."

Walker nodded as he added a sample of sweet onions with scalloped potatoes. She doubted he had any idea what some of the items tasted like. The sauces differed from those of the Southwest—sweeter and tangier, although some could light a fire.

As Amy suspected the two seats remaining rested further along the table. She felt like she needed to sit with her group, acting as a hostess. Anyway, the conversations livened up her days as talk of life on the various continents gave her a world-wide view from her island perch. She doubted she'd ever live on the mainland again. Visit, yes. There were a few places in the world she'd like to explore but with whom? A tour group most likely. Many reputable ones had stayed at her B & B, giving her five-star reviews. One of those would satisfy her travel urges.

Her elbow accidentally knocked Walker's arm. Heat inched its way to her cheeks. "Sorry. I forgot there's not a whole lot of wiggle room."

He grinned between bites. His dark hair streaked with blazing strands from the torches around the area hung long in handsome curls. "It doesn't bother me. If I scoot too close, it's because I don't want to bump a stranger."

"Well, you owe me a nudge or two." Setting her fork on her plate, Amy pushed it out of her way. Soon, a waiter would take it out of sight. "Usually, everyone gets a dessert or two, to savor during the program. I also grab a fruity drink."

Walker patted his lips and chin with his napkin. The candle-light from the floating votives dusted pricks of silver in his light-brown gaze. After hundreds of guests, why Walker? Why now? His hair? His eyes? His hands? What was her attraction? She needed to make a pact to avoid close contact such as meals and evening walks. But what about school meetings, excursions, and breakfast? Some distance even then could be managed. *Yes, I'll work on it. Then the electrical pricks will cease.*

When she made her way to the dessert table, Walker veered for a larger plate and another beef satay and fish taco. He must have found some favorites. Cutting in line, he joined her by the guava cake and bread pudding, bubbling with bananas foster sauce, her favorites. "You can try them all." She giggled, wondering where he'd find room. "The coconut pudding and upside-down pineapple cupcakes are good choices too."

Walker peered at her plate. "I think I'll have what you're having."

Without the turmoil roiling in my chest. He can enjoy his food without these silly butterflies.

Somehow, he managed to save his dessert for the lively, exotic entertainment. Would rubbing his belly be out of place? Looking around he noticed many had turned their chairs to face the stage, stretching out their legs and relaxing from the lethargic reaction to all the food. Would he ever crave the spices of the Southwest or the Mexican fare after months of delectable seafood and sauces over various meats? Perhaps not. He couldn't think of one Polynesian restaurant in Albuquerque. Shouldn't there be a Tahitian community in New Mexico if not in his city? He could try his hand at cooking some favorite dishes. Would Maki or Amy help him? There should be plenty of time for culinary lessons.

Amy adjusted her chair beside his. He'd been careful to focus on the storyteller and not Amy's fair features. In the dark, all he saw were random filaments of light in her hair or flames reflecting in her green glance. Enough to distract him from the performance. What if she decided to quiz him?

She reached across him for her dessert. "I don't know if I trust you by my sweets." Putting a forkful of spongy guava cake in her mouth, Amy concentrated on her plate.

His hands rose in surrender. "I don't know if I can eat what I have."

The steady drumbeat increased in volume and quantity. Flood lights dimmed, leaving the dinner guests surrounded by the flames of the torches. His heartbeat took on the rhythm of the ancient tone pounded by skilled hands. He hoped the beat mimicked a heartbeat or he was in trouble. How long would it take to adjust to a normal *thud thud* in his chest? This dramatic beat pulled him into the motions of the actors on the stage. At least, he hoped they were actors and not ghosts from the past. The painted faces and skin with outlines of tattoos reminded him of pictures in history books or *National Geographic*.

Chants in an unknown language to Walker and humming intensified as men and women covered the stage—the men wearing leggings and no shirts or a skirt-like garment. The women wore short skirts with embroidered blouses, appropriate for the audience, not the ancient story plot. A male and female off to the side, hidden from the limelight, told the story in French and English, as the actors and dancers mimed the story of the creation of the islands.

As an archeologist Walker knew many ancient Polynesian cultures had a version of the story. A god lived in open space, the sky. He created a rock or a mountain that split into many stones and cliffs and corals, forcing the earth and sea to come into being. He created man and woman and placed them where fresh water flowed. Where there were voids, more islands popped up.

This was exactly what Walker wanted to study about these early people. Their beliefs, lifestyles, cultures, how they existed. The unfolding of the world in front of him through dance, fire, and music expressed the accepted oral culture. An archeological dig would give the stories roots.

Amy sniffled. He'd forgotten anyone else's presence. He set her dessert plate on the table and gave her a napkin. How many times had she seen this particular enactment? Still, it brought tears? Though not teary, he did concede a sense of awe and reverence at the beauty and poise of the people and the story.

With the colonization by the French, many forms of paganism had been replaced by Catholicism or Protestantism. Very few pagan rituals remained, perhaps in the deepest part of the jungle of the South Pacific or remote islands. He'd seen no sign of the ancient practices here. Even the remaining tribal villages had advanced in their spirituality.

Yet, the beauty of the performance pointed to God, the Creator of all people and lands.

Bravo, God! Your beauty reigns here.

9

*A*fter a few days of research at the National Library on Laumua, Walker braced himself for the students arriving this afternoon, the first Monday of the program housed in the old barn. Kato and Amy steadied him as his strongest supporters.

I can do this. The students are shorter and foreign or I'm taller and foreign. Either way, I hope to teach them something valuable about their culture and anthropology and archeology. Maybe spark an interest in their past instead of accepting what others tell them. Lord, give me one or two who want to learn more. Show me how to draw their interest, not to me, but to what You want me to accomplish. Amen.

Armed with maps, books, and sketches, Walker arranged his assigned table with colored pencils and paper at all the places. Amy described the first session as stations. He remembered his girls talking about stations in grade school. The students would be divided into groups, most likely by age, and change tables every fifteen minutes. Walker shuddered. Not much time to make an impression. Could he be more nervous about a passel of youngsters than a room full of young adults? Well, yes, he had chosen college-age students for a reason. What did he know about this age?

Amy tapped her fist on the podium. "I see a few worn and weary faces out there. Remember, today we are only giving the students a taste of what you want to share with them. Not all of them will choose your subject. We don't want them to only be interested in, let's say, woodcutting. Luke might end up with four or five with a keen interest. The only one we want to have one hundred percent participation is the choir and music because of the Christmas program."

Her eyes, though making contact around the room, landed and remained on his longer. Could she sense his urgent plea for help and fear of failure or desire to flee? "Smile, have fun, and remember you are giving these darling children an extra boost in their education. If you don't mind, I want Pastor Logan to pray over our efforts."

She nodded to the minister, standing by his table loaded with microscopes and jars. "Father God, more than anything we want this school to be Your school. Lead these students and their parents that You want to gain a unique path toward a bright future. We are Your vessels. Fill us now and let Your love overflow. Amen."

The huge log barn echoed with the prayer. Walker acknowledged if this were a God thing, then he need not worry about the results.

At three o'clock on the first Monday in September, the doors opened to admit not the fifteen to twenty from the previous year but an astounding number—thirty-seven children ranging from six years to sixteen. Walker searched for Amy near the door. Her hands covered her mouth as her eyes glistened with surprise. Or was it awe?

Sitting on wooden benches in the middle of the barn—he must remember to call it a *falea'oga*—the children gave their respectful attitude toward Amy. They were not nervous, for many had anticipated this opportunity. They were not the newcomers—he was. The advantage rested in their court, not in his degrees and experience. He had a distinct feeling he would benefit more as a student than a teacher or *faia'oga*.

Thank You, Lord.

Would he even be able to return to his university classroom with its wealth and resources and huge brick edifice? It dawned on him at that moment that these children and this program encompassed his research. It would not be a paper for the university or a magazine article. He planned to live this research, not print or hypothesize about an outcome.

His growth linked with their growth. He'd learn as much or more than the children would. As the groups scattered to the first stations, Walker chuckled, for his role swiveled from teacher to student as five dark-haired, bronze-skinned little people stared at him.

Words. Use my words.

"I'm Walker, and I'm going to show you some big words and how to explore your world and make a difference. Ready?" These nine to ten-year-old boys and girls nodded. Big golden-brown eyes popped as if he held a surprise in a magic hat.

Instead, he held up a poster with ANTHROPOLOGY spelled in big bold letters and another with ARCHEOLOGY. "We are going to recreate your history. Ready?"

"Yes, sir." "*Oui.*" "*Bien sûr.*" "How?"

After six more groups shuffled around the tables, Walker understood the vision that Amy and her friends held. It really didn't matter if no one chose his class next time because the big picture tendered the hearts of each leader. Whatever the students carried away from their time under this roof would be enough. No performance scale or grade.

I get it. This is not about me at all.

Amy winked at him after the last child left and mouthed, "Thank you."

Lodging the hamper of food securely into the back of the jeep, Amy checked once again for the essentials—water, food, first aid kit, blankets, cell phone, and camera. What her official role was on this trip alluded her. But she couldn't pass up the time to ride through the jungle to the southwestern peninsula of Alexandre. Kato and Walker had handled the planning, and either they invited her or she invited herself to tag along. Having an interest in the archeological dig on the Duprée plantation rang true. Yet, catching up with Lisette posed the greater pull. Their children had attended school with Joshua locally and at the National School on Laumua. Amy's husband, Neil, and Jacques Duprée had become fast friends. The tie strengthened even after Neil's death. Perhaps they felt a desire to watch after her at first. But through the years developed a lasting love and friendship.

Walker strode toward the Jeep with a few more items for the tool chest—a machete, short shovel, and heavy-duty clippers. He grinned under his straw hat with leather straps tied under his chin. "I don't quite know why we need a machete but my boss, the *ali'l*, insisted."

She laughed at the city guy. "Kato can be a bit bossy. Welcome to the jungle. It looks tame around the house but vines as big as your leg might halt our progress. Better to be prepared."

He peered over the back of the seat. "Is there enough room for you? I'd offer to trade you for the front seat, but there's no way my legs would fit in the back."

"No, I'm fine. I can do anything for half an hour."

"It amazes me how close everything is here. At home, we can drive for hours and never change scenery or see another person or a house."

"That's island life. It took me a while to get used to it. If you are claustrophobic, the smallness could be a problem." Amy checked the bags next to her. The ropes would hold them in place. The supplies consisted of items Kato delivered once a month. Even on the same island, the Duprées seemed as secluded as some of the other islands.

Walker's attire matched Kato's—long, green cargo pants with a sturdy, long-sleeved shirt. Boots, instead of sandals. Her own pants were made of breathable material, allowing the breeze to cool her. The fabric somehow absorbed the sweat and dried quickly. Once home she would quickly change into lighter garments.

Amy didn't plan on walking much today. She'd take pictures, listen, and help Lisette. Walker and Kato could tackle the dirt without her assistance.

Kato took his place behind the wheel. Amy adjusted her seatbelt and settled her hat firmly, knowing the windy drive would dislodge it to fly behind her soon enough. Walker tested all the straps again before climbing into his seat. He draped his arm on the window ledge.

If she were excited about this venture, what level of enthusiasm would Walker emit? She had momentarily forgotten he had excavated in Egypt, Greece, New Mexico, and other places. Did digs differ in level of excitement? Making it personal—was one of her paintings more rewarding than another or one garden plot more beautiful? From experience, the one she worked on presently gained her amazement and anticipation. The same with a sunrise or sunset. Or a yellow and red hibiscus or a bird of paradise.

The memories are precious but the present brings life. A reminder to live.

The island road paralleled the beach, sharing spectacular views of cliffs falling into the sea. The land, witnessed through jungle vegetation, formed the base of a mountain range gracing the center of the island. The lush green covering disguised the once active volcano, now dormant yet full of life.

Tapping Walker's shoulder, Amy suggested he look to his right. "High in the trees are colorful lorikeets, a native bird. Even though they are different colors, they are the same species."

He lowered his sunglasses. "I've seen some from my room. They sing a lovely song."

"*Oui*, unlike the croaking of the tree frogs and cawing of the warbler. It took me a long time to sleep with the cacophony of noise. Now, I appreciate it as a symphony and probably couldn't sleep without it. As soothing as the waves lapping."

"Well, my window is open every night, and I've had no problem falling asleep."

He sure was fitting into island life. Could he live on the *motu* of Alexandre? How long would his enamored state last? Hers never wavered, except for a few months when faced with the decision of staying or leaving after her husband's passing. Her family pushed her to come home while her heart and Alexandre Island pulled her to stay. Surrendering to God's plan proved the winner. Since then, she never doubted that this was home.

Kato slowed as the road veered to the right. A less traveled road continued straight. He pointed straight, explaining his route. "If you ever want to have a wilderness experience, straight ahead you will find some national park land with campsites, trails, and a unique off-road adventure."

Walker slapped his hand against the window ledge and perked at the suggestion. "I would like that. Perhaps we could plan an outing for our students."

Kato nodded. "I think the older ones would enjoy that. Many of them live in villages just a step above wilderness though. They could teach us some survival lessons."

"Student-led education is a viable form of learning."

Amy garnered great potential from the conversation. An

additional level to add to the program. "Let's do it. Of course, it would take lots of planning and many chaperones."

Walker turned his head, just making eye contact with her in his peripheral. "If you want their parents involved, this would be an area to investigate. They would have an arena of confidence apart from the standard ABCs and math."

She clapped and rubbed her hands together. The wheels of potential turned. Parental involvement with a student-led project. "I think we're on to something."

Walker raised his hand for a high five from them. "I hope you are taking copious notes and are documenting everything you do. If you need funds, this is the stuff organizations, including universities, love to support."

Letting her pent-up excitement loose, her words spewed with steam of imagination. "Oh, we do need more financial support. Funds and teachers. We have the ideas and the goals, but the momentum stops with the blockade and reality of our limits. We've talked about including other islands."

Walker's side grin reached his eyes. "Let's get it down on paper and see what happens. I know some people."

Laughing, she added, "Who know some people."

"Exactly. One step at a time."

The cut-through took them into the jungle and over a slight rise to the beach on the west side of the island. The peninsula jutted to the southwest on the Pacific Ocean side of the island. The landscape burst with rugged, wilder formations and sharp points and edges. Cliffs, rock formations in the water as small islands, dunes, and ridges. The waves rushed with immense force, similar to the untamed fashion in California and Oregon. The huge expanse contrasted with the calm seaside of Amy's establishment. How could she forget the fearful, unforgiving coast just miles from her home?

At least the Duprées' place was inland with no developments for miles. Amy knew it had some appeal, for Lisette and Jacques had lived here for over twenty years. Jacques' family even longer, since it belonged to his grandparents. His parents had moved to California, thus passing the inheritance to Jacques.

Walker leaned his head out the window. "Is that their place? It's huge."

Kato stopped the Jeep. The lane was lined with palm trees, towering into a canopy. On either side lush, thick vegetation reached toward the beach. Coconut and banyan trees swayed in the breeze. The house spread its girth, almost looking over the orchards beside it. Twice the size of Amy's house, of the same style and age. Impressive and stunning with the mountains rising behind it. She knew that fields of cash crops of taro and sugar cane stretched to the base of the mountains. Other acreage full of fruit trees made this one of the most active plantations on this island and possibly the others too. True farmers for generations. Huts and buildings scattered about housed the faithful workers who were able to rear their children here with the surf-lapped beaches and rainforest wreathed mountains.

Poking Kato's shoulder, Amy yearned to see her friend. "Let's go. We'll be able to enjoy the views from the house."

Amy didn't envy Lisette and the upkeep of the enormous estate. La Maison Cachée suited Amy's needs just fine. If she didn't have guests to share it, it would be too grand to keep.

Opening the Jeep door before the vehicle came to a complete stop, Amy had her foot on the ground ready to race up the steps. A tall blonde woman in a long flowing dress opened her arms and embraced Amy. Once a month registered too long between visits.

"Lisette, it's so good to see you." They were of the same age, though their backgrounds differed with nationality. Each year in the islands erased more of the dividing line. Would she ever truly be an islander? Maybe after fifty years.

Her friend kissed each of Amy's cheeks twice, the French gesture Amy had failed to embrace so far. It's not that she minded, but it didn't come naturally to her. Hugs were a different story.

"Oh, how I miss following our sons around the football games. How is Joshua? David says they are having a grand time. I hope that means lots of studying."

Amy shook her head. Studying or soccer? How quickly they had to change their terminology from international football to American soccer. Hmmm. The question of studying hung in the balance. "Well, you know how the three boys managed in high school—sports and study. I'm hoping no, praying they are practicing a man-version of that life. Mark is probably the most stable of the three. He'll make them study." Mark was the student who played football as a social game.

Lisette linked her arm through Amy's and pulled her toward the house. Would Kato take care of Walker for a few minutes? Lisette probably didn't even notice the men by the Jeep. So much for introductions.

Amy missed the travel to Laumua with the Duprées. But the couple remained busy with their two younger children, Jacqueline and Emeline, both homeschooled at ages twelve and ten. If Neil had lived, maybe Amy would have had other children.

Don't go there. You have the school children. What if's never lead anywhere nice.

Heavy footsteps followed them on the tile floor. Kato cleared his throat. "Excuse me, Madame Duprée."

Lisette pivoted, releasing Amy's arm. "Oh, Kato, I'm sorry. I only had eyes for Amy. Please join us, and we'll find Jacques. And...who is this?" Lisette volleyed her gaze between Walker and Amy.

Amy knew her friend had questions lurking behind her crinkled brow. *Please don't ask them in front of him.* "This is Dr. Walker Standish. I think Kato asked your husband to show him around the dig site."

"*Ah.*" Lisette's French accent made the sounds appear as if admiring a painting. More like awe. What did she see that Amy had missed? "Jacques needs little encouragement to show the grounds. I think we are joining them with a picnic."

"*Parfait.*" Amy had hoped to be out of doors observing and listening to Walker. Would this be worthy of his time and research? She didn't know if he had to account for his time away from the university. "I brought a few things from Maki for the meal, and of course, your produce from the market."

"*Bien, merci.* Anytime we can save a trip, it means more work can be done here."

Amy tilted her head, gaining Lisette's attention. "You know you don't always have to work. A little down time might give you more energy. You could come spend the day with me. Bring the girls."

Lisette chuckled. "Tell that to Jacques. He runs a tight ship here. But I see a day at your place in the near future." She placed her finger against her temple and grinned.

They walked through the house to the back veranda where refreshments awaited them. A long table faced the pool and a garden of exotic flowers. A heavy gardenia scent filtered from the vegetation. Companies had tried to bottle the fragrance without success. Nature had the recipe.

Lisette chose a chair from one end, motioning for Amy to sit next to her. Walker and Kato filed in beside her, leaving the other end for Jacquess. Everyone faced the same luscious view.

"Help yourselves to the macadamia sugar cookies and apricot crisps." Lisette poured sparkling limeade into chilled glasses and passed them around.

Always looking for new recipes and hostess skills, Amy asked Lisette about the apricot concoction.

Soon after every cookie disappeared, Jacques, a man of medium height in his late forties with strength evident in every muscle, joined them. His skin held a permanent tan, almost like a native.

"Kato, I see you have brought me a professional this time, not one of Amy's ordinary tourist or city folk." Jacques extended his hand.

Kato laughed and shook Jacques' hand. "This is Walker Standish."

Walker stood and received the host's hand in welcome. "Nice to meet you. I hope it is no trouble. If anyone says archeological dig, I'm ready with a map and shovel."

The older man nodded, returning the comment with a smile. "Glad to hear it. We could use someone like you. I dabble in the field but have no formal training. Occasionally, I have university groups come, and I get another load of coursework under my belt. I'm always surprised that the locals do not have more of an interest in their heritage. We've had some fantastical finds."

"I'm anxious to see what has been done."

Jacques kissed his wife and embraced Amy before he settled and consumed his share of the replenished treats and his drink. "*Allons-y.*" He glanced at Lisette. "I assume the supplies are ready."

Her elegant cheeks lifted. "If you mean the food, then *oui.*"

The Jeep zigzagged behind the mini-Suzuki carry truck. Walker held fast to the handle above the door, determined to keep his seat for the bumpy ride. Passing dense jungle ferns in the rugged interior, he wondered what naturalists and bird watchers would think. People, like him, traveled thousands of miles to feast their eyes on the exotic island lore. While the Duprées and the Lees inhabited the vibrant, floral scented land--islands suspended in paradise.

A large mud hole jolted Walker back from his analysis. He'd cherish the friendships and would garner exceptional research before returning to the red mountains of New Mexico.

"How long have you known the Duprées, Amy?" His raised voice carried over the bumps and hard-working engine.

She leaned forward, making the transition of her voice easier to understand. Her wayward tendrils of hair touched his face. He didn't mind that or her hand braced close to his shoulder. He forced his hand to stay by his side instead of reaching for hers.

Concentrate, Walker, you asked her a question.

"About fourteen years. Neil and I attended a Christmas party at their plantation. That sealed our decision to buy Maison Cachée. If another couple could live on a remote island and prosper, so could we."

"So brave."

"And young and naïve. Joshua was three. I don't know what I would have done without Maki and Lisette." Her voice trailed to a whisper.

"Did you ever think of returning to Oregon?"

"Yes. Grief wrapped tightly around me. I desired to flee but couldn't move. My son and this island became my cocoon until I got my ability to fly again."

Walker understood the paralyzing grip of grief. This sabbatical symbolized his wings to fly. Yet, his flight seemed selfish compared to Amy's journey with a small child and no extended family. Her strength and confidence buoyed him. Perhaps in another eight years, his equilibrium would return, or sooner? Six months melded in the island culture might be the cure God prescribed.

A metal gate marked the boundary of the archeological site. Private property. He'd read that most of the island's historical sites and digs were privately owned, although many of the relics were turned over to the government and placed in the national museums or local ones.

As he set his feet on the ground, he considered the exercise an honor, walking in the footsteps of the original inhabitants. A steady drumbeat echoed in his mind. The ancients lived through their descendants. He grabbed his professional camera, joining Jacques in front of the truck. Kato and the ladies flanked them.

Holding up one side of a map that Jacques produced, Walker willed his jaw in place and listened as Jacques pointed with his free hand. "We know a lot about this site. The bold lines show the building we've uncovered and the dotted lines depict what we think is there."

Counting in his head, Walker saw fifteen edifices with detailed dimensions and architectural markings. "Wow. You have a village."

"We do, complete with the stone seat used by the tribal leader. Smaller stones formed a semi-circle, most likely for the lesser leaders or representatives from each family."

Walker pointed to a mound in the far corner. "And this? Could it be a burial cave?"

"Yes. A true treasure."

Archeologists labeled a burial site as a treasure trove. "You can find out a complete history of a tribe by the burial site. The tricky part is treating the whole process with reverence. Even pagan graves deserve respect and delicate consideration."

Jacques nodded. "We follow all of the government's guidelines, which I've heard are international too."

Amy stepped onto a path and began a winding journey through the roped off grounds. Walker dropped his side of the map and watched her form, imagining a citizen from five hundred years ago, walking the same route and taking care of family and neighbors. Humans from every era formed their care groups and made life work together.

On impulse, he followed her, desiring to see the sights

through her eyes. Her hand dangled by her side. He reached for it and squeezed her fingers. "Mind if I walk with you?"

She paused, staring at his hand linked with hers. He withdrew it. He hadn't anticipated his handholding action. "Sure. I have lots of questions, and you have the knowledge. But first, I want to stroll the site and soak in the thoughts that someone lived here centuries ago, loving her family, cooking, playing, crying…all of it."

They wove through the village, not veering off the path, eventually choosing the one leading to the burial cave. Both of them halted. The open cavity should be a place of peace and hope, so why the hesitation for both of them? He visited the cemetery at home a few times a year. The sunny, open grounds lent a tranquil, steady vibe. But here?

Reaching for Walker's arm, limiting his advancement, Amy whispered, "I don't know about this. It's dark and mysterious. I don't feel God's presence."

That was the difference—the peace derived from God's indwelling, even in a cemetery. "We'll wait for torches to light our way. There's enough other stuff to keep our interest."

Her soulful eyes, dark in the entrance, cleared and sparkled once she stepped back to the entrance. "I'm about ready for lunch."

He nodded and turned. The view from the cave, with a bit of imagination, showed the outline of a well-organized village. "Can you see it, Amy?"

"What?" She took in the panoramic scene slowly from left to right.

"The village. The huts. The people." Some might think his words nonsensical or crazy. Would Amy write him off as foolish?

She nibbled her bottom lip during his survey. A purposeful smile inched upward to encompass her nose, eyes, and forehead. As if a movie reel spun its pictures, she stared, then pointed. "I do. There are four huts sharing a common courtyard for washing and cooking. Around the corner are more huts, some in groups of three, some four. Across the path is a larger gathering hut for women to weave or sew while gossiping or bragging about their children."

Walker followed her scenario. If possible, she had a clearer rendition of village life. "*Oui, ma chérie.* That is why archeology is rewarding. The world gets an opportunity to step into the past and conjure up true meaning."

Waving to Lisette across the town, Amy moved slowly in her direction. "I've always been fascinated about this culture." Clasping her hands behind her back, she perused the landscape. "I do wonder if these people appreciated the lush, fertile land."

Chuckling at the image of an ancient people enjoying a sunset or building sand castles, Walker connected to her questions. "I think God imbedded an innate awe within us to contemplate and appreciate nature. Unfortunately, these people worshipped the creation not the Creator."

"Hmmm. Until the French came with their missionaries."

By the time Walker and Amy joined the others, a table and chairs had been arranged in a work hut. Sandwiches and fruit rested on paper plates by the two hampers. Between Lisette and Amy, the cold lunch menu more than sufficed. They could have fed five more people.

Jacques pointed to various boxes and chests in the room. "We keep supplies and utensils under lock in case of unwanted trespassing. The last thing I want is someone getting hurt. We have waivers for any diggers to sign." He crossed his arms on the table. "I was thinking, Walker. Why don't you come stay a while? We can give you a room at the house or a cot out here."

"Really? I would love that, especially if there is a certain area where you need help."

"I'm wide open. This project will never end, so you would have free-range. I have an extra carry truck for your use."

Walker rubbed his hands together. "When can I start?"

Everyone laughed. What? Too eager? This was his candy store or race track. And he really wanted to drive one of the little trucks.

Amy folded her paper napkin before putting her plate in the paper bag. Of course, she was happy Walker found a project. Never did he say he wanted to laze around on the beach or read around the pool all day. He had too much energy and mind to do that. But why was she hanging her head? Surely, she could last a few days without him.

He's a guest with time on his hands. His island sojourn has very little to do with me.

Lisette added the rest of the trash and bumped Amy's shoulder with hers. "Why so glum?"

No comment. She could deny it, but what excuse was there for her downcast countenance? Easy fix. Amy glued a smile on for the conversation. If only Lisette would drop her raised brow and quirky grin.

"What's with you two? You haven't finally found someone attractive, have you?"

"Shhh." Amy glanced over her shoulder. "No, nothing like that. We are friends."

"And how many male guests have you been...uhm...friends with over the years?"

None, and Lisette knew that.

"We have mutual interests, and he will be here for half a year. I might as well treat him as a friend. Breakfast everyday with an acquaintance would be unrealistic."

Lisette refused to remove her smirkiest facial contortion. "So, this friend, in just two weeks, has joined your school as a teacher, assisted you in an excursion, needed your help shopping, eaten out with you, and now visited your friends. I'm just waiting for a dance and a kiss."

Amy's jaw dropped as she glared at her friend. "You are unbelievable." Lisette's imagination was truly extraordinary. Too many hours in those Christian romances.

Pivoting with her nose in the air, Amy marched to where the men studied a huge map of the village stretched between two poles. She made sure Kato stood between Walker and her. Their planning weaved in and out, mixed with Lisette's observation and Amy's denials.

A week apart would cement her purpose once again—one that did not include Walker beyond his departure date. She fanned her face with a spare paper plate. What happened to the breeze?

It vanished with her friend's words.

10

Construction work on the barn began in early October. Local residents, many of the students' parents, contributed labor hours. Donations from local villagers supplied the lumber and flooring.

Amy stood in the entrance, watching the loft transition into useable space with sturdy steps, instead of a ladder-like structure. The office and storage space would relieve the lower level for needed classrooms.

Draining her cup of tea, Amy placed it on a table and put on gloves from her back pocket. Time for physical labor—a bit out of her league, which usually consisted of walking or jogging. Lifting and hauling pushed her strength limits, though she was willing.

"What do you need upstairs?" She knew from other attempts that shouting proved her best option in the big facility.

Walker leaned on the rail, his wide smile catching her off guard. Of course, he would be helping. Every day since his return from a week at the dig site, he'd poured himself into aiding the school, physically or mentally, while reserving a few days for research on Laumua. Honestly, she'd missed his daily presence that week. But by the fourth day, she'd forced him into a compartment in her mind without easy access. Or so she thought. When only the smallest thing reminded her of him surfaced, he crept to the forefront.

"A box of nails and two of those boards." He pointed to a stack of one by eight boards.

Amy giggled, for the brilliant professor couldn't recall the sizes or names of the construction items. She stood by the pile of freshly cut boards—half the length making it easy for her to haul. "These? Are you sure?" She couldn't help herself. She ribbed him about his lack of speaking knowledge with basic terms.

He hit his forehead with the palm of his hand. "Someone needs to put a sign on each pile."

Stuffing a box of nails in her tool apron, Amy hoisted a board on each shoulder and slowly took the steps up, balancing her load carefully.

Walker met her and placed the boards next to the wall. Bending down to catch her attention, he commented, "You know I could have gotten those myself. I just wanted you to join me up here."

Reaching in her pocket for the nails, she occupied herself with the mundane. Why would her presence demand his subterfuge? "Really? I can't imagine what skills I have that you need."

Chuckling, he moved her to the right side of the loft where her office would be. A sheet hung over a wide expanse. "I hope you don't mind, but the guys and I added something to the plans with Maki's approval."

If everyone approved, it must be a good thing. "Oh! Let me see, please. I feel like I'll love it." A painting? A shelf?

Walker removed the sheet and let it fall to the floor. The dramatic act revealed a wide window, allowing sunlight and a breeze to infiltrate the area.

"How perfect. Thank you. *Merci.*" She bounced on her toes and threw her arms around his neck, blocking out the sense of other workers watching. "I was wondering if I'd feel claustrophobic up here, but now I will experience the outside world all the time." When his arm circled her back, she forced her arms to her side. Her touchy expression of gratitude ended. A bit embarrassing and very spontaneous. She'd need to be careful. Looking behind Walker, she shared her enthusiasm with Kato and Luke. "*Merci beaucoup.*" Although they didn't get hugs, she hoped she covered her *faux pas.*

Walker turned her shoulders to the opposite wall. "There will be one here too."

She held onto the rail instead of a repetition of transferring her excitement on Walker. She did catch his stare, his blue eyes communicating something she didn't care to name. "Thank you, Walker."

"My pleasure." He squeezed her shoulder, winked, and returned to work. Work for her—no for the school. Just because he wanted to give to the community. Surely, it had nothing to do with her personally. She could be ninety years old, and he'd act the same. Right? Well, maybe not the wink.

The physical labor was not something Walker would say he gravitated to on a normal day. Books and a walk around campus required no lifting or exertion. Even his regiment at the gym failed to use the muscles he discovered while building the loft. Even though his body rebelled and pushed back, his core accepted and craved the challenge.

Once Amy returned to the house, Walker set his course on the project. Luke, a master in his craft, taught Walker and Kato how to rout and angle the boards for a polished touch. His words encouraged Walker to trudge onward. "In a few more days, we'll be able to see our finished product."

Before Luke had time to start his drill, Walker heard a piercing, "*Allo!* Is anyone up there?" The shout reverberated around the room. All three of the men shrugged, not recognizing the feminine cry.

Kato stood and peered over the rail. "*Nous sommes ici, Madame.*"

"Ah, Kato is that you?"

"*Oui,* Brigitte. *Un moment.*"

Kato turned and whispered, "Brigitte Gavin from the village."

Walker didn't remember the name, for he'd met so many people. He'd rather continue working in order to finish in a few hours. Both men looked at him. Luke added, "Nothing is as it seems with Brigitte. Walker, you need to be wary of her motives."

"What motives? She doesn't even know me or know what I am up to, does she?"

Kato headed to the steps. "I'm not so sure. She has a plate full of sweets. I don't think she's bringing those to me or to Luke." He clicked his tongue and shook his head.

Sweets for me? Why does he think that? Walker's instinct circled around, hiding in a corner or behind the sheet. At forty-four he should not feel threatened by a squealing, cookie-carrying woman. Anyway, the men could be wrong.

Marching down after them, Walker had a few seconds to assess the woman. Yes, he had met her at church. Tall, blonde, early thirties, pretty as a model, not an eyelash out of place.

"*Tiens,* Walker Standish, it's so nice to see you again." Her syrupy sweet voice bypassed the other men. "I brought you some homemade cookies."

His smile faltered at her gooey, sweet words. "Miss Gavin, is it?"

"Why, yes. You remembered."

Why did he repeat Kato's words? It would have been better to feign innocence. No, he hadn't remembered her, not really. Bad slip.

His friends leaned against a table with their arms crossed, watching and snickering. He needed help, and they weren't budging. Perhaps they'd been in her spider's web before. The plate of sweets levitated to his chin.

"*S'il te plaît*, try one." Brigitte eased closer.

Walker took one and stepped away. Tempted neither by the cookies nor the woman, he occupied himself with a bite, nodding his thanks. Was it a competition? There was no game nor race for his affection. What Brigitte expected he wouldn't want to find out.

A flash of turquoise entered the barn. Would Amy rescue him? Her token was a pitcher of lemonade. Her steps faltered as she laid eyes on Brigitte, hovering close to Walker.

Practically running toward Amy, Walker side-stepped the platter of cookies and found shelter next to Amy. "I'll put that on the table for you. *Merci*. Just what we needed."

Observing Amy's rigid stance, he deduced her stunned by his quick, awkward actions. *Get a hold of myself. I'm not a teenager caught in a casual flirtation. I'm not flirting at all with anyone. Look, I'm sweaty, unkept, and a would-be-carpenter. No catch at the moment.*

Using Amy as a shield, Walker gulped a plastic cup of lemonade, occupying his hand and his mouth, washing down a dry cookie in the process. Brigitte sashayed toward them. He gulped and inched near Amy's side, wishing for glue or Velcro, anything to stay out of Brigitte's clutches.

It didn't work. Walker was paralyzed. Deep breaths steadied him enough to remain on his feet. A panic attack? Now? He could run. At home he'd excuse himself from the crowd or uncomfortable situation and shelter in his house. It wasn't always an interested woman who sent him scurrying. Crowds could have the same effect. Ever since Rebecca died, his social tolerances waxed and waned. On reflex, he grabbed Amy's arm, someone to ground him from a predator, albeit a harmless one.

Amy jerked her head up toward him, as she questioned his actions. In his brown eyes, darkening each second, she detected fear—uncomfortable, darting, true anguish. Her own anger wilted, replaced by words instead of stunned silence.

"Brigitte, thank you for dropping by. What a surprise. May I help you with anything?" Walker squeezed her elbow with a nonverbal grateful pulse. "Your cookies look amazing. I'm sure the men will enjoy them. Why don't you put them on the table?"

Brigitte's mouth puckered. "Why, Amy, I thought you'd have something to do inside such as paperwork. I can handle these gentlemen, especially Walker." Her hazel eyes darkened with a high school crush. Or jealousy?

Amy rose on her toes and laced her hands in front of her. "Well, I needed a break."

Brigitte's manicured nails drummed on her chin. Nothing good could come from that conniving squint, stalking Walker. Amy refrained from proclaiming her guest as off-limits. Instead, she should be thankful for Brigitte's interest. A crush from someone for Walker could work to Amy's advantage. If his heart shifted toward someone's affections, she could release her growing attraction for a man exiting her life soon. Brigitte wasn't the one, but Amy could find someone else to spend time with Walker.

That could work. Why add a man to my life after twelve years? I don't know the first thing about Matchmaking 101, not with a guest whose future is four thousand miles away. I'll have to pray about that. Right now, Brigitte needs to take her model-self elsewhere.

Taking the plate from Brigitte to the table, Amy linked her arm with the woman and tugged. "Why don't we go to the veranda? You can tell me all about your trip to Hawaii."

"But...I..." Brigitte glanced at Walker, who had put six feet between them. His eyes softened and his grin returned.

He understood. *Bravo, Walker. You owe me one.*

He winked at Amy, as she pulled Brigitte toward the open barn doors. Amy would pat herself on the back later. Now, to entertain a gossipy acquaintance and produce a list of appropriate matches for Walker.

$\mathcal{W}$alker dodged the entanglement with Brigette because of Amy's influence. Could he manage on his own? For he could hardly expect Amy to hang on his shirtsleeve ready to protect him. After church today, he had a business luncheon with the director of education. Since meeting her, he hoped business was the extent of the rendezvous. The Brigitte fiasco shook him a bit.

Sitting next to Amy at church in Laumua had a calming effect, natural and peaceful. Knowing all she wanted was friendship eased his frantic nerves around women. She'd lasted this long without a husband. Surely, he could conquer the single life too. People did it all the time.

Not taking her eyes off the worship leader and praise team, Amy tilted her head, almost touching his shoulder. "This is what I wanted to hear. Nadine thinks our church could have a small worship team on Sundays. Maybe even involve some of our students."

Tuning into the message in song, Walker connected with the words. Hymns and praise songs inspired him to worship. Focusing on God sure was a better use of his time and energy.

"Wonderful idea. The Christmas program is a fine example of what she can do."

Amy nodded. Her emerald green blouse complemented her green eyes, bringing out gold specks. He drew his attention back to where it should be. Better yet, he closed his eyes, letting the melody and words penetrate his wondering mind. Focus. Purpose. If only God would tell him exactly what to do.

Walker apologized once again for making lunch plans. Amy didn't mind. The Sunday market hosted many food trucks. Used to fending for herself, she waved goodbye to him, promising to meet him at the pier at four o'clock. Turning around, she caught a glimpse of a dark-haired, trim woman, grasping Walker's hand. She could almost hear the laughter from here as their smiles radiated familiarity and common ground. He had said it was business with the education department. Although the woman's clothes favored the professional with a navy-blue jacket and high heels, her casual greeting sent jealous shivers through Amy.

Jealous? Of Walker with another woman? Pish-posh. Maybe I won't have to consult my list after all. This woman might be the one. Good, right? So why the knot in my stomach?

Hunger. Feed me and all will be fine.

She bought a fish taco, her easy go-to, and sat at a picnic table in the plaza. The market buzzed with shoppers and casual browsers. Families with children and couples holding hands. As a younger woman, she had hated eating or shopping alone. Not anymore. At some point she had accepted her aloneness.

Taking her shopping list out of her bag, Amy decided to tackle it before finding a bench in the park where she'd read. She'd have to find a book first, one of her favorite shopping chores. The floating book mobile didn't come often enough for

Amy. Today, she'd refurbish her supply of novels. After she read one, she'd put it in the library for the guests.

"*Bonjour*, Monsieur Talbot. *Comment ça va?*"

A wrinkled older man rose from behind a stack of books. "*Ah*, Madame Lee. *Ça va très bien. Et vous?*"

"*Bien, merci. Bien sûr, j'ai besoin de livres.*"

He stretched out his arms. "*Il y a beaucoup.*"

Lots of books in seemingly disorder. Although Monsieur Talbot could skim titles in a matter of seconds, his order appeared chaotic to Amy. Yet he knew his clients and pointed her to a row of books picked out especially for her, if she didn't know better. If she had the time, she'd love to help organize the heaps of books. She always thought she'd make a good librarian.

"*Merci.*" A new mystery or an inspirational British historical. If she needed an old favorite for a reread, her own library over-flowed with classics and her favorite authors. What would Walker like to read? Did he bring his own reading material? Enough for six months? Was it all nonfiction, technical research? That sounded so boring. How can you curl up with a textbook?

Her fingers stopped their stepping on the top of the spines. *Do not think about him. The books today are for my pleasure.* No matter how many times she told herself to shove him out of her thoughts, he crept back in, perching on an inconspicuous shelf. She'd bypass that category and replace it with plans for the B & B or the school. Her tangible projects proved more faithful friends than her heart endeavors. The sooner Walker settled into his friend compartment, the better for her focus. Perhaps his lunch date would become a love interest, freeing Amy from unnecessary scenarios.

"I'll take these, *s'il vous plaît.*"

Monsieur Talbot checked the titles. "*Ah, bon.* Good choices. I've heard this Laura Franz book about Scotland is a fine read."

"I love the title: *The Bound Heart.*" At times her heart felt bound to the past. Maybe the characters had a happy ending.

"If you and your friends like *The Lady's Mine* by Francine Rivers, let me know, and I'll pass the information onto others."

"I will. She never disappoints." Amy searched the counter for any new island books. "Is this a good guide?" A drawing of the seven Suamalie Islands in a dark blue sea popped on the cover. She examined it closer. "I know the writers. They stayed at my B & B a year or so ago. Nice couple."

Monsieur flipped through a copy. "I haven't looked, but you might be in there."

That would be nice. Any free publicity in a reputable book would help secure her place in the tourist industry.

The owner rang up her purchase, processed her credit card, and placed her books in her reuseable bag. The weight of her package lightened her step since she knew of the hours of entertainment the books would provide. If she didn't have other items on her list, she'd find the park bench right away. Instead, she found her favorite candle maker at Flames-A-Glow. One hundred percent local—no American or European brands here. Thinking to resupply a few scents for the common rooms, Amy chose gardenia and hibiscus.

"Amy, it's been a while." Beth motioned her over to the enticing lotions and soaps. Though not on her list, the bins in the supply closet could use a few more items for the guests' rooms.

Amy adjusted her bag, getting heavier by the minute. "How are you? I didn't see you at church today. I don't come to the Laumua often on Sunday. How are the kids and Tom?"

The petite, olive-skinned woman had adorable girls that visited a local Alexandre festival with their school each year. Amy tried to see Beth often on her forays to Laumua. "The girls are with Tom at the beach watching a volleyball match. They both think that is the sport for them. We'll see. High school is just around the corner. I can't believe it."

Believe it, my friend. "It zooms by." Amy brought a circular soap wrapped like a flower to her nose. "Ummm. What is this?"

"My own concoction—rose and mint."

"I love it. What color is the soap?" She matched the soaps with the towels in the different bathrooms.

"A soft pink with red specks from the rose petals."

"I'll take a dozen if you have them."

"I certainly do." Beth produced a floral bag and placed the items on a bed of tissue. "By the way, Tom has a friend from his law firm..."

Amy's hand went up palm out. "Stop right there. I'm not interested."

"But you don't even know what I'm going to say."

"I don't? Let's see. 'He's very nice and has a good job. He's divorced with two grown children. I think you would get along just fine.'" Amy giggled as her friend shook her head and shrugged. "Am I right?"

"Yes. But if you ever want to branch out a little bit now that Joshua is gone, you know who to call."

"Who? Your husband?"

"Well, how about lunch one day with me instead."

"Now, that is a date." Amy glanced at her watch. Just enough time to pick up a few art supplies before heading to the park.

By three o'clock she had her favorite hot tea with just a bit of sweetener and a sweet berry pastry. Her bench faced the less populated part of the beach with a view of the pier.

Her new historical novel laid in her lap, but the sun's warmth distracted her, lulling her eyes closed beneath her sunglasses. The lapping of the waves, the shouting of children, and the steady beat of a drum and purr of guitar strings altered her cobweb brain into a well-swept place of comfort. Now, she pulled in deep breaths, making room for love—the kind of love God offers for all His children.

That's what I want at the Maison Cachée. Room for love. A place where guests can find rest and hope and love.

Do I have room for love?

She sighed and stretched out her legs. Her book fell to the ground. Before she could retrieve it, a man picked it up for her.

Shielding her eyes from the sun with her hand, she muttered, *"Merci."*

Walker laughed as he turned the book to see the cover. "It must not have been very entertaining."

She righted her slouching posture. "Ha. I wouldn't know. I didn't open it."

Walker gestured toward the bench. "May I?"

"Bien sûr, monsieur. How was your lunch?" *And your date?*

"Productive."

That could be taken many ways. Did he come to the islands to find a new love? She refused to ask what he meant. Either he wanted to share or not. Beth had stirred up too many questions and awkward suggestions. His playful grin might depict he was evasive on purpose. Surely, he didn't think she was jealous or nosey. Anyway, he wouldn't know that she'd seen him with a woman.

"Dr. Landon shows interest in furthering anthological study of the islands. With some research and proposals, the Suamalie Islands could be brought to the forefront of the French government as well as financial investments from other countries. But we have to be careful with the number of tourists and participants at the sites."

She locked her gaze on his, hoping he could not see her concern and myriad of questions under her sunglasses. She had no standing among the educated in that field. "Well, Dr. Standish, what is your role in this endeavor?"

Crossing his arms and leaning back on the bench, Walker

removed his shades, giving her full access to his eye language. Truth and openness. "I don't know for sure at this point. We are getting the communication channels open. The logistics will be worked out over months or even years. Sometimes, these projects have a way of stalling or coming to complete halts. The main concern is the size of the islands. This will not be a tourist attraction. Purely educational for now."

"Hmmm. So, someone in Dr. Landon's position is needed to proceed. She must have some pull higher up."

His forehead crinkled and the boyish grin returned. "Yes, *she* does."

Oops. He hadn't told her Dr. Landon was a woman, had he? He draped his arm along the back of the bench and chuckled. "How did you surmise that Dr. Landon was a female?"

"I...well, I saw you at the café." She yanked her sunglasses off a little too dramatically. "I was curious." How was that for honesty?

"Curious, but not jealous?"

"Certainly not. With whom you dine is none of my business. You are a guest with freedom to entertain anyone you choose." Would fanning herself with her book be too obvious?

"Precisely." His pause irked her as he played with her emotions. "By the way, she is married with two children. I'm positive there is nothing to be jealous about. That is, of course, if you were."

Suddenly, she remembered how it felt to be thirteen again. "I wasn't," she whispered. "Are you ready to return?"

He stood and replaced his sunglasses. "Ready. Do you mind if I stop on Alexandre to pick up a light supper?"

Before she could stop the tumble of words, Amy murmured, "I have leftover lasagna, if you want to join me. It would save you the trouble."

"Lasagna? I haven't had Italian in weeks. *Oui, bien sûr. Merci.*"

"Have you been working on your *français*? Your accent is improving."

"*Un peu*. If I stay long enough, I'll have a working vocabulary of what, maybe three hundred words?"

She grinned. And even longer, he'd master the language perfectly.

Oh, she would kick herself later. Walker, her friend, was coming to dinner. Nothing more or less.

12

The early morning colors danced through the open windows into the kitchen, lighting a path for Walker, one straight to Amy with her hands busy putting some kind of icing or glaze on the muffins. Normally, Walker waited on the veranda around nine o'clock with the other guests. But after their late night, he wanted to lend a hand.

He knocked on the counter, preferring not to startle her or Maki. "*Bonjour, mesdames.* Is there anything I can do to help?"

Amy smiled then darted a glance at Maki. Or was it a plea? Maki shrugged, leaving the decision to Amy. "Maybe. How are you with scrambled eggs?"

"The fluffiest and lightest in Albuquerque."

Her attention returned to her glaze. "I don't believe that, but you could prove me wrong."

Walker strode to the sink and washed and dried his hands. Amy handed him an apron with huge daisies decorating the front. "I hope you don't mind a few flowers."

After tying it in place, he looked down. "I've avoided the flowery clothing so far. As long as no one takes a picture, I'll be fine." The huge hibiscuses on the others' aprons weren't a better choice. What about a plain white one?

Maki handed him a bowl full of eggs. "But you are so handsome, *Monsieur*. I have an idea to snap one right now."

As he cracked and whisked the eggs with milk, Amy stood close and added cheese, spices, and sausage. She smelled like gardenias in the summertime, fresh and light. Understated but noticeable. Her voice rose just above a whisper. "Did you get enough sleep last night?"

Following her pattern, he lowered his voice to match hers. "Hmmm. After talking till midnight, I would say no, but I'll manage. You?"

"Like a baby. Just enough." She blushed, or her cheeks flushed from the work.

"Luckily, I'm free until the children come after school. I can take my book to the beach for some languid sunlounge lying."

"Oh. I like that expression. Did you coin it?"

"No. A guest wrote that in your B & B book. I loved it."

Walker presented his scrambled eggs for inspection, although there was no way to unscramble them. Amy set the warming dish on the counter. They looked appetizing to him.

"Thank you, Walker. I can count on one hand how many times a guest has helped in the kitchen." She exchanged a chuckle with Maki. "Do you remember Mary Ann from Georgia?"

Maki set pineapple chunks on the fruit platter. "I sure do. She wanted to add biscuits and gravy to every breakfast. So, for seven days straight, she joined us here and made a batch of extremely good biscuits, Southern-style, she said."

Shaking her head, Maki looked at him and pointed a finger. "We don't want you coming in here disrupting our stream-lined routine." Although she stated it with a smile, he felt sure it contained a serious warning.

His hands shot up in surrender. "Warning heeded. I'll not

sprinkle your fare with southwest spicy seasoning either. As long as you will ask me to help if needed."

Maki nodded in agreement. Surely, Maki and her husband had vacation or left the premises sometimes. What about Amy? Did she ever have time off?

"Amy, do you ever take a vacation?"

Her hand swished her hair from her eyes. "Someone once said living here is a vacation. But to answer your question, the B & B is closed in January every year."

Her words jolted his body to a rigid stance. His wide-eyed stare captured hers. "But…"

She held her hand, palm out, in front of her face. "I know what you are going to say. You are an exception since you booked for so long."

He had no idea. "But how will you go on vacation?"

"I promise, if I decide to go someplace, Maki and Luke can run this place for one person. Even Nadine could do it. Don't worry. As for now, I will be here. I'll need the time to regroup after two weeks with Joshua home."

How could she be so unselfish? He'd think of some way to make the time special for her. May he would cook her breakfast for a month or make her lunch often, or…

Whoa, Walker. She might not want any of that. Or she might! Which would be worse? I'll see what the next few months hold. By then, she could be tired of me.

He hoped not.

Today, Walker had his same six students who chose to work with him once a week. Their keen minds and interest made Walker question why he taught in higher education. Sometimes, he'd go through a whole semester with only a few questions and not near the amount of enthusiasm. These students, three boys and three girls, challenged him to rise to their level of curiosity. After all, their ancestors most likely lived in the ancient overgrown villages. If he could help them unearth pieces of their history, he'd do all he could. He had spent many hours, pouring over maps and old records in the national archives in Laumua.

He studied the eager faces that seemed to hang on every word he said. No pressure, right? "Today I have a map from the archival library. Well, it is a copy, of course. Let's move your books and papers and spread this out."

Aolani, a ten-year-old, helped Walker roll out the map, securing each corner with a stone from the archeological chest. "I don't recognize all these outlines." The boy's observation and attention to detail amazed Walker.

"That's because this goes back to the 1700s. People didn't have the tools that we do now. No satellite views or measuring devices. So, let's see if any of you can find some landmarks on Alexandre Island."

The treasure hunt began. They listed some semi-familiar locations, including their village, the B & B, the school, beaches, caves, the jungle, and lagoons. They were having to guess because the shape of the island resembled two maracas with their handles attached in the middle.

Marie, an eight-year-old, dark curly-haired girl who spoke with a French accent, guided her finger to a black dot not far from where the present-day B & B plantation was marked. "What's this?"

Walker had seen several of those markings on the map. After researching, he assumed they were caves like the one at the Duprées. "A cave, I think. We can ask Kato to be sure." Well, nothing was sure with an old map that looked like a musical instrument. He would use his current map of Alexandre and overlay this one to be more accurate. That was another lesson after he located tracing paper. Not anticipating the melee of really excellent questions, he came unprepared for that task. At least he knew they understood the purpose of a map for tracking landmarks and distance. Even though inaccurate, the map's original use as a guide proved authentic.

With his waving hand, Walker motioned to Kato. The young man had a rapport with the children that Walker could never have. Kato, being a native, appeared like them and shared the same deep genetic roots to the land. Some like Marie had French heritage, too, but any percentage of native blood gave them an advantage. Enviable in Walker's vantage point.

"*Bonjour. Avez-vous une question?* I'll see if I can answer it." He obtained a seat next to Walker and peered at the upside-down map.

"Marie, ask Kato your question."

The little girl beamed her perfect smile, first at Walker, then Kato. "I want to know what this black dot is so close to the house and barn."

Kato leaned over and walked to the other side of the table to get a clear rendering. "Ah, it is a cave."

Marie puckered her lips and crinkled her brow. "I don't see a cave around here. How can it disappear?" The other children nodded with the same quizzical expressions.

"*Donc*, it is still here." Kato pointed to the south through the windows. "I've seen it and taken a few steps inside. It is hidden by the jungle. As far as I know, it has never been explored."

Never? Or at least not recently if it is covered and not discovered? Walker stared open-mouthed at his friend. "You mean to tell me Madame Amy has a cave on her property."

"*Oui, monsieur.* Don't appear so surprised. The hills and mountains have many of them." Kato's titled grin reeked of "gotcha" play.

"I know, but one so close might contain relics of the past. It is an archeologist's dream project."

Kato shrugged. "It could be much like the cave at the Duprées' plantation. I don't know. Years ago, my friends and I were scared to go very deep inside. And now the entrance is covered with vines and shrubs."

"There you have it, children. A hidden cave." Walker's spooky, dramatic voice rendered wide-eyed stares and dropped jaws. "But please do not wander into any unfamiliar spaces. It's not worth the risk. Right, Kato?"

Marie's large brown eyes peeked up from the map to Walker. "Will you try to discover what is in the cave?"

Would he? "That depends on many elements, which is a good lesson for next time. What does it take to open an archeological dig?"

Studying the old map, Walker let his finger tap the ominous black dot. A cave. *What will Amy say? There's no way I can let this pass. Curiosity by itself will get me in trouble.*

His gaze traveled to the loft where Amy breezed between the easels, teaching her art students. He'd give himself time to formulate a plan. If he started talking now, his boyish enthusiasm would jumble any cohesive thought patterns. He'd wait until his professional jargon and thesis formulated. He straightened his table, securing his maps and books in the chest. With one last glance at Amy, he grabbed a notebook and pen, heading toward the beach. He'd scribble some notes and clear his mind with sun and a swim—almost a cure-all. Island medicine.

The nap on the beach Amy had envisioned never happened. Instead, she carried her sketch book to the far edge of the back garden, choosing a lounge chair away from guests, though they tended to stay closer to the house. Her eyes tried to see what they saw, perhaps a jungle full of wild animals and creepy insects and snakes. But the years trained her senses to the truth. With no poisonous snakes or insects, the jungle floor posed no threats. A few large flying foxes known as fruit bats could be intimidating with their three-foot wingspan. They could be seen day or night, harmless to humans, instead preying on insects and vegetation.

Facing the jungle and the mountains, she sensed the life stirring in the trees and crawling on the ground. She chose to gaze upward to the trees, just in case a ground mouse or rodent scurried nearby. Those creatures could stay away deep in the jungle for all she cared. Catching the reds, yellows, and greens flitting among the foliage, Amy settled her pencil in its familiar hold. Color would come later from memory.

The detail of the lorikeet, elusive at first, arrived when the bird and its friends decided on a nesting place in a golden shower tree with orange trumpet vines laced over the branches. Brilliant rays of sunlight showered the scenery with dancing sparkles like a Christmas tree with blinking white lights. The gentle song of the forest aided Amy's fingers, bringing life onto the paper.

How long had it been since she had produced a sketch or a painting? It didn't count as she taught and aided students. Too long. Over the past twelve years, a few attempts of the ocean, flowers, or wildlife dotted her sketchbook. What made her yearn to fill the entire book with her art now? Was her heart finally healing, opening up areas dormant for so long? Too long?

She searched, much like she did for the colorful birds among the briars and vines of the jungle, for the loneliness and fear she kept close for years but could not grasp now. Shouldn't she feel it more with Joshua gone?

I sought the Lord, and He answered me; He delivered me from all my fears. Yes, Psalm 34 has been answered. For this moment, I am free of my prolonged fears. Thank You, Lord.

Her heart was as free as her hand now creating beauty from the jungle. Somehow, she made the birds sing on the page. With color the black lines would pop with resilience and hope. They weren't afraid on their perches in the trees. More so should she have confidence to fly and land joyously in the midst of, well, whatever life gave her. She did have some choices. Opening her heart to friendship, or to love, now seemed possible. Why? She was unable, or unwilling, to pinpoint. It was just so.

Sketchbook tucked under her arm, Amy chose the far path circumventing the house toward the beach, amazed at the diverse views available on her tiny piece of the earth. As the waves drew her through the shrubs, the salty air began its healing and cleansing. She dropped her sketchbook on top of her sandals before running to the water's edge. Her knee-length skort would survive a few splashes.

No sunset on this side of the island. But the burst of fading flames reflecting off the sea was a show of beauty she never tired. The golden blaze sparkled orange, red, and pink on the water it descended behind her. God's light shone every day in his universal creation.

Turning toward the pier, Amy saw someone relaxing or sleeping on one of the beach Adirondack chairs. She loved seeing her guests, and even wandering tourists, to appreciating the bountiful beauty. The turquoise seas spurred daydreaming. The simple ways of South Pacific charms suggested sit-on-the-beach and read-a-book holidays. If only she chose more often to give into the local south seas' idyll ways. Maybe she would add a siesta in a hammock tonight. Or better yet, a good book curled up in her big round wicker swing right beside the outside doors of the library.

A long arm reached out in a wave. *"Bonsoir,* Amy." Walker swung his legs to the side, sitting with his elbows on his knees.

"Well, professor, what have you found to occupy your evening?" The table held a book and a drink, her two favorite pastimes—nutrition and entertainment.

"I found a local history book. It was very interesting before I fell asleep. What is it about the air here? The breeze lulls me toward laziness."

Amy sat on another lounge chair. *"Oh, pas du tout, monsieur.* The islands do not consider taking time to connect with nature as laziness. Legend says these are healing waters, and island time takes into account our connection with the elements. This is a guilt-free zone." She spread her arms out encompassing the dazzling coastline, the mist-covered mountains, and the jade forests. "Anyway, your reading material lacks the page-turning element."

He chuckled as he tapped the cover. *"Au contraire.* For what I have in mind, it's perfect. Would you like to grab a taco and let me share what my daydreaming produced?"

Did she? Why not? Curiosity would drive her to his side at some point. "You can't drop that nugget and leave me hanging. I'll grab my shoes."

Walker on one side and the glowing sea on the other whipped hints of unearthed blessings.

Barfoot Café offered the fare they sought along with the gentle cadence of the sea. Walker's glances alternated between the boats on the water and Amy's pretty sun-kissed face. She never needed any make-up. In fact, he only saw glimpses of manmade enhancements on Sundays. Even then she tended to add a little mascara and lipstick. Island life agreed with her. Did it agree with him?

More and more.

The pull from Alexandre Island's core nudged him. He wasn't a naturalist or humanist. Yet, he did believe God placed a connection between man and the earth, as He told man to cultivate and care for it. Anyway, the spark of change motivated him to wonder.

The coconut crisps disappeared before the two plates of

shrimp and rice with mayo sauce appeared. They had both gravitated to something other than fish tacos.

Amy leaned over her plate and took the first bite. He enjoyed watching her as her eyes closed for the savory ritual. Licking her lips, she confirmed his suspicion. *"Parfait.* The chef here knows how to please. Aren't you going to try yours?"

He nodded, remaining speechless. How silly to be enamored with someone eating. Well, not just someone. Amy. He didn't watch the guests at breakfast each morning, although he heard them. Quickly, his attention toward Amy would become obvious and an embarrassment to both of them. He directed his attention to the spicy aroma awaiting him.

The flavors in his first encounter with the new-to-him dish blended so well that he couldn't concentrate on one particular spice or taste. What ingredient served as the bond, creating a whole new flavor?

Letting his fork rest on his plate, Walker hesitated before he reached for his mango coconut drink. "I don't want to erase the perfection as you called it. What makes this dish so unique?"

"Ah, mon ami, if Raymond told everyone his secrets, we wouldn't all race back for more."

"Well, I don't think I'll ever order anything else here, except maybe his fish tacos. They are truly awesome."

When the food vanished, Walker pushed his plate aside, grabbed his drink, and leaned deeply into his chair with one heel resting on his knee. Amy had finished minutes before, sparing a few bites of her dish. "I'm glad we get to walk home." Home? "I never do that in Albuquerque. Rush and eat and work or watch TV."

Amy swished her drink, mixing the remainder, and crinkled her nose, adding a goofy smile. "You know there is a TV in the great room."

"I know. My mind doesn't need it anymore. I'm cured. The same with social media. Since Wi-Fi is spotty, and I'm not complaining, I avoid the social element and use it for research and communicating with my daughters. They are upset that I don't send more pictures."

"Hand me your phone. I'll get a shot of you and the ocean."

He dug in his pocket for the device, put in his passcode, and handed it to her. "Megan will be your friend for life."

Three photos later, he flipped his camera for a selfie. "Now, one of us." She scooted closer. "Two smiling faces and the glamorous background with the stars and torches lighting a dance floor across the sea."

Amy twisted her shoulders and head to offer a full stare. "A bit poetic for an ordinary night."

The boyish part of him wanted to hold her chair beside him, but the insecure man let her move it back into position. *Mon amie* she would remain. For now. One thing he did know, he would not be sending that picture to his daughters. It wasn't worth the questions.

Amy held her glass up for a refill. Fruit drinks could easily serve as a dessert. "Tell me about your plan or your investigation. I'm a good sounding board."

Walker accepted a refill too. Adjusting his chair to include the beach and Amy as the center point, he processed his words. All he had to do was ask with no harm done. "I'm glad, since it has to do with your property."

The twinkle in her green eyes contained an openness and interest, possibly excitement. At least he detected no negative vibes. After all, who was he to suggest what she could do with her own estate?

"Do you know there is a cave not far from the house?"

She nodded. "Kato told me a few years back. Neil and I had no idea when we bought the place."

"Kato says it's overgrown and no one would know it's there. It must seem like the side of a hill or mountain. With little effort, we could clear a path and gain entrance to see what you have. It could be no more than a few feet inside. But I don't think so. Little Marie asked about the black dots on a map today. They denote caves. One corresponds to the Duprées' cave and the others I'm sure would be similar. If someone in the 1700s marked this one as a cave, then it is significant, not just an opening."

Elbows on the table, drink forgotten, Amy focused on every word. "What are you suggesting, Walker? That I might have an ancient burial cave?"

His enthusiasm rose at her grasp of the scenario. She didn't react as if she were against the idea of exploring. Well, she didn't know what "it" was yet. "Yes, or a dwelling. Either way, it is ancient, probably used at the same time as the Duprées'. I don't think the French explorers had much use or idea about the caves. Archeology was not at the forefront of their mission."

"Well, what are you waiting for? Let's get our shovels and machetes and start the search."

His laughter probably reached the other tables. "Who are you? Miss Indiana Jones? Whoa, Amy. It's not that easy."

"Oh, I know. Government permits and all. But that is for the future once we explore a bit, right?" With her bouncing in the chair, he expected her to spring up and tackle the exploration tonight.

"Are you a secret archeologist?"

She winked. "Maybe."

"I have a book to loan you." He held up the history of the island.

"You forget, Mr. Jones. It's my book. I've read it."

"Truly? I thought you said it was boring."

Shaking her head, dragging her curls back and forth across her shoulders, she tilted her head. "No. I said it wasn't good reading-a-book-on-the-beach material. But for garnering information while studying, it is perfect."

"*Bien, mon amie*, let's make a plan."

"I'm all in, shovel and all."

Walker put the Suamalian *tupe* next to the check. For once Amy did not argue about him paying. This place had become a part of him. Now a local dig. What more could he ask for? He even got a walk along the beach by the calm *sami,* a sea of promises. In another time, he might even have clasped Amy's hand.

13

---

ll in. What am I thinking? Amy giggled like a school girl wanting to play on her brother's baseball team. The main difference was Walker encouraged her to participate. As she had done for him at the beginning with his beach attire, he picked out her "dig" clothes—steel-toed boots from the shed, a hard hat, canvas overalls, and a construction apron, which she owned. The overalls he presented were for a taller, larger person but worked with a belt and a thick rolled cuff.

Glancing in the full-length mirror in her room, she admitted the outfit could serve in the Amazon jungle or a trek down the Nile too. No flowery skirts or billowing shirts with sandals and a straw hat.

Walker and Kato waited at the shed where at least half a dozen tools lined the outside wall. Walker appeared in charge as he pointed to a tool, but Amy knew Kato had a keen knowledge and experience with island excavations. No PhD but sometimes common sense and strong work experience could suffice.

Amy pulled gloves out of her apron, put there by Walker. No garden variety ones today. "Okay. Go ahead and laugh." She posed with hands on her hips. "And then, don't you dare make fun of my attire again."

"Yes, sir. I mean, ma'am." Walker high-fived Kato at their near simultaneous remarks.

She bowed, hoping their teasing stopped soon. Anyway, they dressed much the same, except their clothes fit. "What do I need to carry?"

Kato picked up a machete and a backpack. "Do you think you could carry our water and energy provisions?"

Energy? Wasn't this cave no more than half a mile away? What could happen?

Kato continued, "And this machete for path clearing."

"Of course. Thank you for clarifying, I wouldn't be killing big rodents or wild animals."

Walker chuckled. "No, we'll take care of those."

While putting on her full backpack, she grimaced at his care-free response that could be true. "Not funny."

Luckily, the plantation had existed for two hundred plus years as a civilized estate. She and Neil had little clearing to do. Basically, she maintained and monitored the grounds instead of fighting back the elements. Perhaps, the machetes would be limited to plant species, not hissing, howling, or biting ones.

Professor Standish, exposing his professional training, clicked off some rules. "We all stay together, meaning no heroics or glorified single conquests. Wear your hard hats at all times. Make sure the machetes are cutting away from your bodies. If we dig, use shallow holes to avoid breaking anything beneath the surface. Call for help if something feels wrong. And, try to have some fun. You are explorers. Who knows? You might be the next Indiana Jones."

"Yes, sir." Amy and Kato agreed in unison. Her response dripped with sincerity and seriousness. All his points held validity.

They walked in silence to the edge of the cultivated yard and chose a trail guests used for a more rustic hike. At a giant banyan tree, Kato pointed toward a hill in the distance at the foot of the mountain. "That's our destination," he paused. "I think."

Amy wondered at his lack of certainty. "You think?"

Shrugging, he winked at her. "Well, I was a young teenager when I found the cave before. So, I'm reaching a decade back. My memory is lagging, you know, old age."

Walker motioned to his own head. "Ha. You have no idea about old age."

Oh, to be young again, joking about old age. She certainly couldn't remember such details about his thirteen-year-old self, much less hers. "Now, I know we are on a true treasure hunt where a dot marks the spot on an ancient map." At least, she knew a nice comfy home awaited her. This wild jungle would not be so wild. She could be in her back yard in thirty minutes —unless there was a way to get lost with these two jokesters.

Not every archeologist stood as Walker did on the threshold of discovery as the first to enter an unexcavated site. True that what lay within could be no more than a shelter with a ledge as a covering. But it could be so much more.

His heartbeat thumped as the *thud thud* on a log drum—deep, constant, heavy, full of anticipation. Kato and Amy allowed him to make the first hacks at the entrance. Behind the trumpet vines, thick wisteria, and massive Tarzan-like jungle vines, he saw a cavity instead of more dense foliage. Definitely, an entrance of sorts. Chances were good that a myriad of chambers wound into the mountain, natural or manmade by the ancient natives. No bears or wild cats on the island, so he didn't expect any surprises of wildlife attacking him, unless a hairy rodent or massive spider spooked him.

One more whack and the entrance appeared as the curtain of time pulled away. Kato and Amy flanked him as their cord of three waited for the play to begin. A moment of awe ascended unscripted. He reached for Amy's hand without losing sight of their discovery. Lacing his fingers with hers gave the moment a healthy dose of reality. Squeezing her hand convinced him he wasn't alone, and he didn't *want* to be alone anymore.

"Wow!" Was that all he could say?

Amy searched him, her eyes glistening. "I don't even know what I'm experiencing here. But 'wow' or 'awesome' comes to mind."

Kato cut some more of the vines, giving the effect of curtains tied with sashes. The young man used his words, which Walker couldn't find. "It appears to be some sort of dwelling for man, not beast. Look at how the entrance has been carved and rounded. Someone took pride in making it sturdy and useable. These studs are solid." Kato pounded his fist on one.

Releasing Amy's hand, Walker followed suit and knocked on another wooden stud. "Built to withstand a cave-in. If someone went to all this trouble, the cave must have had some kind of important use."

Over the years as he taught and encouraged his students, Walker learned to read faces and determine interests and intention. Reading thoughts helped determine the success of a venture. Well, he wouldn't label himself a mind reader, but he did know the questions rambling through a novice archeologist's brain. Amy's stance, as she leaned inward while keeping her feet outside the cave, declared curiosity with a healthy dose of wariness. She wouldn't be the one bursting ahead into unchartered paths and halls. What a relief!

Setting his backpack against a wall, Walker pulled out his flashlight. "A few reminders before we move forward. Take your flashlight and loop the string around your wrist." He lighted his helmet. "Make sure your helmet is secure. As we move forward, don't be in a hurry. We're in this together, and no one is in a rush."

Amy adjusted her strap under her chin. Her big eyes registered excitement much like going on a whitewater rafting trip for the first time—willing but cautious. "What will we see? I've only been in caves in Kentucky and Tennessee as a teenager."

"I doubt we'll see stalagmites and stalactites. If the Duprées and others on the islands are our examples, the rooms will be open and roughly cleared, mostly at the level of the entrance."

Clapping her hands, Amy readied her flashlight. Kato claimed the back position, while Walker led the parade. "Ready? *Allons-y.*" He winked at Amy and saluted his rear guard.

With three beams of light, the entrance danced with life as darkness fled. Unlike many abandoned caves or dwellings, this one housed no debris or signs of recent occupation. No squatters of human or animal forms. It was as if nature had sealed it from any maleficent use.

Mentally, Walker wrote his script for his journal—preliminary measurements and shape. "Right or left, team?"

Amy shrugged and turned to Kato for an answer. "How about left?"

Walker aimed his stream of light in that direction. A six-foot-tall arched opening accessed a well-worn stone path. Soon steps led a few feet up toward another room. Walker could guess the purpose of this room by the circular shape and the altar-like table running the length of the far wall.

The professor in him asked a probing question. "What do you think this room was?" All three stood facing the table, their flashlights crisscrossing the space.

"A meeting room."

"A ceremonial room."

Amy, then Kato, supplied their guesses. Walker cocked his head toward them. "How did you do that? You haven't sat in one of my classes before. You are both correct."

Amy high-fived Kato, before returning her attention with raised eyebrows. "We're waiting, Dr. Standish. Give us your professional answer."

He chuckled, wishing he had his reading glasses to complete the image. If only all his students were so exuberant. "I think this was the place the chief spiritual leaders held council. The altar would have been used for worship, maybe sacrifices if that was part of their practice. The dead could have been laid here, perhaps in a shroud before placed in the burial chambers."

Amy hugged herself and scrunched her nose. "You mean that all of these rooms are graves?"

There was the wonder he thrived on when students connected with the project. "Yes, ma'am. Will you go in with us?"

"I don't think I have a choice. I'm not staying out here alone with all the ghosts of the ancient priests and gurus."

Kato stepped into the fray, waving his fingers in a zombie-like fashion. "Who goes there?" His deep, theatrical voice boomed. "I'm going to get you for trespassing."

Amy inched closer to Walker without taking her eyes off of Kato. Swatting at his stiff, stretched arms, she howled at him. "I'm not scared of a youngster like you. I'm going to be the one haunting you, if you're not careful."

Quickly, Kato stood at attention, biting his nails. "I'll be good, Madame Lee." His smile sealed the promise.

Walker gained a little control, or at least he thought he did. "The passage leads to the right." His light emphasized an open space with steps leading down. "I'll go first."

So far, he had not seen signs of a cave-in. Occasionally, he noticed braces reaching from floor to ceiling, an ingenious feat for the ancient culture. They could have been from the settlers in the 1700s. As the room opened up, he guided his flashlight from the floor to the walls. The cavern was enormous, the ceiling low—a little under eight feet. Carved out for a purpose.

The mounds and uneven floor spelled out that purpose without a doubt.

"A burial ground," he whispered into the sacred area. How many bodies, he couldn't guess.

Kato's voice echoed around the cemetery. "So, they are buried in the ground."

"Yes. The question is in how many layers? We won't know until a team excavates."

Amy's flashlight slowly shed its light on each section. "Look, there are figurines and pottery around the walls. I suppose the government will need to know about this."

Walker finally let out his awe in a powerful whoosh. "Yes. Even though this is private property, it must be reported and handled properly. You do realize, Amy, this is a wonderful piece of the puzzle of the island's early beginnings. I'd say this piece of undisturbed history will garner lots of funds and research."

"Will it be handled as smoothly as the Duprées' without excessive interruptions?"

Walker nodded. "I think so. If you don't mind my help, I'll see to getting the paperwork, and we'll go from there. It will be a slow process."

Amy surprised him as she found his free hand and squeezed it. Her eyes were dark in the obscurity of the cave. "Thank you for wanting to preserve the island's history. The children and their parents might not know it now, but one day they'll be glad their past is not erased."

His heart raced and his fingers heated as they curled around hers. "You are welcome. It's what I enjoy doing. And with you, I love it even more."

14

The constant change of guests and the influx of new students kept Amy grounded in her comfort zone. Her exploration and bonding with Walker impressed upon her once again to set the boundaries of guest and hostess. She had wiggled across the line on the verge of eliminating the wall entirely. Walker's absence for a few days gave her time to reestablish her equilibrium.

This is why I continue to refuse the romantic interests of men. They are complicated. Well, if I'm honest, no one has impressed me, not like Walker. I've not wanted to walk along the beach holding hands with anyone in over twelve years.

She shook her hands at her sides, releasing his imaginary touch. *When is he leaving? Too long for me to avoid him. Prayer might work.*

Since she was working in her front flower bed, she got on her knees and faced the house, possibly fooling anyone walking the paths. Her hands found familiar warmth from the rich soil.

Lord, I am so confused. My shield that I thought You wanted me to have to protect my heart is broken. Please fix it. Fix me. I have no room for a short-lived romance. Why now? This man, You know,

Walker, is leaving in a few months. Please help me not give away any of my heart. You gave me the strength to live alone. Please return that gift. I don't want to give it up for a silly crush. We'll talk about this some more. Amen.

There. Done. Her request left no opening for a new love. Even a handsome, brilliant, interesting professor. Friendship, yes. Nothing more.

Walker whistled as he increased his stride on the path to Maison Cachée. *Home.* He was only gone for two nights, but he'd missed the cozy familiarity of his suite. Was that all? No, he missed Amy. What that meant he had no idea. Her presence at breakfast or finding her curled in a chair in the library with an open book? Perhaps their occasional walk on the beach or her stance in front of her easel? Analyzing hadn't helped him much, except for losing a few hours' sleep or falling behind on his research. Could he just let his feelings find their own way?

Right now, he yearned to share his new finds with her—not with the university or his daughters. With Amy. He could just say it was because of her interest in the property and nothing more. Where would she be at four o'clock with no after-school program today? He glanced to the left and saw a figure with a straw hat, turquoise shirt, and faded jeans, kneeling in a flower bed. How did she manage to crawl in there without crushing the plants? Carefully, with purpose and control. A lot like how he maneuvered in a dig site, afraid of disturbing a pottery fragment or a bone.

Maybe that is how I should pursue our relationship. I'm more liable to crush what we have in friendship if I zoom into something more.

"Amy."

Her gloved hand shaded her eyes as she lifted her gaze

toward him. "Walker, I'm glad you decided to return." Her smile pricked his heart, adding a rapid extra beat or two. Genuine? It had to be, since she hadn't had time to conjure a fake rendition. "I thought maybe the metropolis lured you into her clutches."

After she pushed herself to her tiptoes, Walker reached for her hand, helping her glide over the flowers. "Hardly. It seems all I need is a suite in your B & B on a remote island. Don't tell anyone, but I even called it home." His daughters would think him crazy. Home was in a faraway house in New Mexico with roots and memories and his family. Right?

Her grin punctuated her cheeks. He had missed her reactions during their conversations. If he read her correctly, she had missed him. "Well, you were sorely missed this morning with the new guests. We had to listen to Mr. Allen from Milwaukee go on and on about his big fish stories. I know you could have added your own stories. The other guests needed you to steer the conversation. I might need to put you on the payroll to divert the awkward, overly zealous talkers as well as the occasional silences."

"You jest. I'm probably and proudly the most boring of the bunch."

"*Au contraire, mon ami.* Your excavation stories and world adventures outrank others since you are a gifted storyteller."

He considered that he might be as overzealous in stories as any other person. He picked up his overnight bag as Amy gathered her gardening bucket. "I really am a shy fellow who just happens to have a few short stories."

"I'm sure you could have your own movies, swinging on vines, fighting serpents and Nazis."

Pottery and graves hadn't placed him in the danger of renowned archeologists. But if Amy wanted to make him a hero, so be it.

Walking close to his side, Amy's elbow touched his arm. He almost linked her arm in his but didn't. Another way he was not a hero in a movie. He did not always have a heroine by his side, except for right now, if she chose the role. He would distance himself at the entrance where space allowed.

After removing her hat once out of the sun, Amy's green eyes formed serious depths. "You underestimate the power of your teaching ability through very few words. In fact, your humility and shyness work in your favor. You, unlike other people, aren't talking to hear yourself speak. Your conciseness supplies needed information in an interesting format. Keep doing whatever you are doing."

He felt his neck and cheeks warm. Having Amy on his side blessed his perspective of what he tried to do with his students. He didn't realize others benefited too. Could he make a difference here in an area rich in history with the locals who had roots and a stake in the information and artifacts? Could he teach them something or at least open their minds to their heritage?

"I sometimes wonder. That is one reason for this sabbatical. Maybe I'll get a second wind and go back rejuvenated." Although part of him toyed with the idea of staying. He planted some seeds this week. Now a wait-and-see game. What would spring out of the ground in a government-based decision might be absolutely nothing or a chance of a lifetime.

Before parting ways in the foyer, Amy pivoted, stopping his forward trek. Her hands, now free of her garden basket left outside, twirled her hat by its brim. Nervous? Of him? "Would you like to come for dinner, and we can discuss what you found out?"

How much did his revealing smile convey? Lately, his calm facade portrayed an unfaithfulness. If he let the wall he'd built around his heart crumble, he was doomed to a season of pain. But as if he had no control, he nodded. "*Oui, merci*. I'll bring the paperwork from the archival and historical monument department." Nothing personal about that. His heart would be safe within the confines of the papers.

In an instant her hat stopped spinning and her mouth formed an even line. Disappointment? By what he said? He probably knew why but dared not voice it. But if she didn't tell him, he didn't have to come up with an excuse.

"Of course. Bring the papers. I was hoping you had some encouraging news. How about at seven o'clock?"

"Perfect. I'd offer to bring something." He chuckled at his awkward position. "But my cupboard is bare."

"All I need is your appetite. I think you'll like my choice. It's hard to make a meal for just one person. Without Joshua, many of my recipes lay dormant. You are a good excuse to prepare one of my favorites."

He rubbed his hands together. "I can't wait. A hint?"

"Nope." She scrunched her nose mischievously and spun toward her portion of the house.

Even with his wall in place, a good day just got so much better. Bits of him decided to rebel, altering his plans somewhat. He had a few hours to pull them back into place. Is that what he wanted?

Her veranda, like half of the guests', faced the pool and the jade mountain. The bamboo dividers, separating her from the others, gave privacy without obscuring the view. A ring of orange, purple, and red entertained any faithful seekers. Amy never tired of the spectacular setting of the sun. It wasn't over the water but the majestic, rugged mountain held its own magic.

She fidgeted with the napkins and silverware, which needed no attention. Gardenias circled a clear glass vase with a white scented candle inside. Too much? Well, she often set the table for herself exactly like this. Walker could think whatever he liked.

As if the thought of his name had power, he stepped around

the divider with two slushy drinks. What more could she want than a handsome, grinning man bearing a fruity smoothie? Not much, except a way back to her simple life from before he arrived.

She accepted his offering. "Let me guess, mango and coconut?"

"You know me well. Ever since you introduced me to the concoction, I keep returning to it."

The frozen, refreshing drink was perfection at the hands of her bartender/pool guy. Although other establishments might offer the alcoholic versions, Amy offered nonalcoholic drinks for her guests. She closed her eyes at the first sip. Perfection. Could she possibly be confusing her taste buds with her pounding heart? She'd seen Walker a hundred times, yet she had this reaction more and more.

Be still my relentless, treacherous heart.

"Have a seat and enjoy the sunset. I have the plates in the warmer."

As she suspected, he followed her into the kitchen. "Ah, it smells wonderful. What is it?"

She set the plates on the counter. "Mahimahi stuffed with shrimp over jasmine rice with a sweet and sour sauce."

"I hope you didn't go to too much trouble for me. But thank you for the invitation." His hand rested close to hers on the counter.

She moved her hand and pretended to wipe it on a towel. He grabbed the plates and placed them on the table while she picked up the tea pitcher and followed. His chair seemed a bit closer than she remembered. For now, they could both see the mountain and brilliant colors as they faded for the evening. So, what if there was a little less elbow room. Sharing the show with someone else with a nice meal was rare but oh so needed. She missed the companionship of her son. At times she could barely remember her meals with Neil.

Walker extended his hand to her. "I'd like to offer a blessing if you don't mind."

Hoping her words remained fluid, Amy said, "Of course, that is fine. Joshua and I always returned thanks."

They bowed their heads and held hands. Walker's voice filled their space as if it had been missing and came home. "Thank you, God, for this time again in this beautiful setting. Bless our friendship and this meal. May we continue to serve You in all things. Amen."

"Amen." Her heart had steadied even while holding Walker's hand. Once released she worked hard to function normally. She served a mixed green salad into two bowls. The olive oil and vinegar dressing mixed in during the tossing glistened in the candle's glow.

Walker began with the main dish and dug in with gusto. Would he even try the salad? "This is a masterpiece, Amy. Before I came to the islands, I'd never had mahimahi. In New Mexico, I avoided seafood, not knowing how far it traveled. I did enjoy fresh catch from the lakes and streams though."

"I'm glad you like it." So glad. She'd made this recipe many times, so she knew she couldn't mess it up.

Between bites they shared news about their children. Her conversations with Joshua centered on all the new things he was experiencing at the university—new friends, classes, grades, and rarely about how much she missed him. The last thing she wanted to stress was her loneliness. If he came running home for her, to keep her company, she'd never forgive herself. She wasn't the first single person to experience the empty nest.

Walker's daughters expressed their concern about him with lots of questions. They had become hovering mothers. Was he eating well, getting enough exercise, resting? Was he bored or depressed? Little mother hens. He laughed at their suffocating concern. Megan expected him to cut his sabbatical short and return to his normal life. Different from her situation where Joshua knew exactly what she did every day.

"Megan doesn't understand that the islands are having the opposite effect on me. I'd be more inclined to extend my stay than abandon it."

Extend his stay? Was he thinking about it? Not likely. He had a fine job and family in New Mexico. In Albuquerque, he had everything he needed to ground him. The roots were deep. This place was just something new. Right? A diversion for a period. She didn't even know the logistics of the scenario of extending his stay.

"She's young and feels a responsibility for your happiness. When she sees you, she'll most likely let go a little more till eventually she'll let you be her wise, old Dad again. She'll realize adults can live alone and be very fulfilled." She sighed, remembering the first years without Neil. Walker was blessed to have two precious *someones* who cared. "Stay put while I bring dessert. Would you like coffee? I have a local decaf blend."

"Definitely decaf, please."

Her logical, sensible self returned as she placed a large portion of coconut sponge cake on Walker's plate and a smaller one on hers. Coconut condensed milk drizzled on top gave it a unique, sugary layer. Amy knew she had found her place in her kitchen, running her B & B. All was fine. Her life needed no one else. She'd listen to Walker's goals and dreams, while holding on to her own. He had a whole world to explore.

I need to listen and encourage without losing my heart. My feet have no desire to roam. I'll live my life content in my little piece of paradise. Joshua has his life to expand beyond the islands. As does Walker.

When Walker eyed the creamy, rich dessert, he licked his lips. With his fork ready, Amy could tell he restrained himself until she set his coffee cup down and joined him.

His boyish enthusiasm over a simple cake encouraged her taste buds to try it as if for the first time. Perhaps she should do that with a lot of things. Seeing with new eyes, even with the eyes of her guests. Wouldn't that make her life fuller and less of a lonely existence?

Memo to self—seek renewal, open my heart, make room for others.

As the sugar flowed through her veins, she used the extra energy to buoy her through the evening. She had a feeling Walker had a few surprises before they called it a night.

Walker sat back in his chair with his coffee gripped in both hands. "This place is so lovely. How do you get anything done?"

She scooted her chair at an angle for a better view of her dinner guest. "Well, I have a business to run if I want to keep the view."

"So true. But you enjoy your work, don't you?"

Her work? Most of the aspects, even the cumbersome guests who sometimes didn't know how to respect the environment, reinforced her spirit of caring and giving. The vibrant colors and the pungent tropical aromas warmed her, covering her with memories, reminding her of why she fell in love with Alexandre Island in the beginning. "Yes, it is rewarding. So many people come here. If I'm able to offer a little joy and relief to stressful lives with a few amenities like a good breakfast, then I've succeeded in my goal."

What did he search for with his darkening blue eyes? She'd answer his questions, if asked. The staring probed beyond casual curiosity. The silence, even for a few seconds, cast a spell. Would he share that part of himself, lurking just out of reach?

He broke the mesmerizing moment with a shudder and a loud breath. "Do you want to know what I learned from my appointments?" Adding a wink, he had her full attention.

Amy pulled her legs up into the chair. "Oh, yes. I can't even imagine getting into offices so quickly."

"I'm shocked, too, because I know of all the red tape in the United States. It would take months. But here, there is not a line of citizens or visitors wanting to talk to the archeological and archives division of the government. Since I had talked to Dr.

Landon earlier, my name had easier clearance. I shared about your property and about the Duprées'. I offered to work through my university, forming teams to stay for three weeks at a time to study and excavate. A team would only be three to four students and a leader."

She peered over her coffee cup, daring him to explain in plain words. If she heard correctly, he could be coming back again and again. "Would you be that leader?"

Please say yes.

"I hope so. The director asked if I could extend my sabbatical to oversee the projects."

There. That is what I wanted to hear.

He captured her wide-eyed stare. Hopefully, he didn't misinterpret. It was not as if she disapproved. "Surprised" would be a good word.

"I told him it wasn't as easy as a phone call. Paper work, details, project portfolio. I'm praying about the opportunity as various ideas saturate my mind. I'll need some time to work it out. It might come to nothing or a smaller version of the director's plan."

"Oh." All she could muster. Did she want him to stay? Wasn't six months long enough? If he left her, life could go back to normal. But was this about her? Not at all. This was his life. "I hope it works out how you want."

He dragged his fingers through his hair and leaned forward with his elbows on his knees. The floor claimed his stare as he kicked at a small pebble. "If only I knew what I wanted. The idea is so new." He reached for a side table and brought a folder of papers to his lap. "These are the preliminary papers to register your cave with the department. I'll go over all the legal hogwash with you. If you want, I'll help with the descriptions. I'm impressed that the government gives you as much control and say as it does. It wouldn't be this easy in the States."

His demeanor possessed all the qualities of a man in control

—a businessman—not a friend. Where was the shared cama-raderie of their exploration? Had she misread his intentions?

Why am I concerned? I don't want him to be more than a friend. A comrade on a shared mission will be all right too. Why don't my thoughts and feelings fall in line? I can't have both—a comrade and a romantic relationship. One or the other.

She accepted the papers and thumbed through them. "I'm sure every inch of the islands holds some kind of ancient relic. Did you feel comfortable with the interviews?"

With his heel now resting on his knee, Walker relaxed into the heavily cushioned seat. She could get used to this casual after dinner repose—so much better than a rigid professor pose portrayed in books and movies. He really didn't seem to be the suit-and-tie kind of guy. Oh, to have easy companionship with someone who wouldn't leave when his stay ended. What was she thinking? He had an agenda that didn't include her. Not much at least. Her cave, perhaps, more than Amy herself.

She flicked the papers in a casual arch. "What is your opinion about the cave and these papers? Be honest."

He reached for her hand. She wasn't quite sure why. Yet, she responded, resting her hand in his. "I would never dream of being dishonest with you." He squeezed her hand, then lightly caressed it with his thumb. "This is your home, your land. The government supports that. If you choose to open it for excava-tion, the paperwork and imminent government approval are there. Honestly, it would be a great hands-on learning tool for your school—history, archeology, woodworking, culture—all a few hundred yards away. Of course, only after it is deemed safe."

Leaning back on the cushion, Amy closed her eyes. His touch accessed rooms in her heart that she thought empty and dead. The chambers had been only dormant, lulled into inac-tivity out of fear and protection. What if she had opened the doors sooner? Would she have married again? Would there have been more children? If so, she wouldn't be sitting here with

Walker. Perhaps he was the only one able to thaw her heart. It certainly wasn't frozen now.

"Okay." She slowly opened her eyes, meeting his solid, trustworthy, hypnotic ones. "Let's do this. Will you help me with the paperwork?"

He winked, laced his fingers with hers, and made a promise she hoped he would keep. "I will, madame. I might even stay as long as you will have me."

She blinked, determined to break the spell between fantasy and reality. What did he mean? When had she started misinterpreting English? He said he *might* stay. She'd lost all common sense and couldn't process his words.

His phone buzzed and vibrated on the table. Her no-phone rule had been thrown out too. Where was the Amy of a few weeks ago? Amy peeked and saw a pretty blonde's picture.

Releasing her hand, he groaned. "It's Megan. Do you mind if I take this?"

"Not at all." She uncurled her legs and started the ritual of picking up the dishes. She understood about grown children. Oh, so hard to ignore their calls. What if something had happened? Babies, children, adults—it didn't matter. Parents would always be parents, no matter the age of the children. She prayed Megan was all right.

Walker rose and stretched, walking the length of the veranda with his phone to his ear and gained some privacy. She vacated his space and deposited the dishes in the kitchen. Although concerned, she never wanted to be the person listening in on a conversation. From what she had gathered from Walker, Megan wanted to organize Walker's life, tell him what was best, and wait for him to bend to her will. The conflict arose when he listened but then did what he wanted instead. He was, after all, a grown man and her father. Thankfully, Joshua had not reacted that way. *Yet.*

As she finished clearing the table, Walker's pacing landed

him in earshot. "No, I will not do that. You are welcome to come here. Pouting will not work. I'm staying."

Amy disappeared into the kitchen again. She'd eavesdropped, albeit accidentally, long enough. What did she know of parenting willful, young women? What did anybody know? When she was younger than both of his girls, she'd disobeyed her parents, married, and moved halfway across the globe. Her poor parents. By Megan's age, she had Joshua and her idyllic island home. Perfect until Neil died. Gone was her fairy tale existence. Maybe Megan and Lucy would have more stable young lives.

Walker's shadow crept over the countertop. "Sorry about that. Megan feels she needs to check up on her wayward father. How could I dare enjoy my sabbatical?" He braced himself against the counter, hanging his head. When he peered up through his dark lashes, he grinned, shaking his head. "She thinks I'm crazy. She wants me to admit defeat and come home. Now. When I hinted I might stay longer, she let me have her full-strength lecture. I have a feeling she'll be here at Christmas to prove to herself that I need to come home. No one ever warned me about babies growing into adults."

Amy side-stepped toward him and pinched his cheek. "You poor baby." Her silly voice severed the serious waves. "As if you needed to be punished for disobeying."

In a matter of milliseconds, Walker trapped Amy between him and the counter. His hands rested on the marble, while his forehead touched hers. *No, no, no.* Would he kiss her? *Yes. No.* Had she played too much?

With no rhyme or reason her hands went to his shoulders. She bit her bottom lip and peered up at him through her lashes. She met dark and shadowy eyes. What had she done? Wayward and guilty as well.

"Oh, Amy. I've wanted to kiss you for a long time. But I don't want it to impact our friendship."

She hadn't kissed a man for so many years. Well, maybe a peck on a few dates. But a real kiss? "Maybe just one kiss wouldn't ruin anything."

A deep, guttural laugh preceded his warm breath. His hands covered her cheeks tenderly. He studied her face, her forehead, cheeks. Her eyes failed her as they pricked with tears. Since when did tears accompany a kiss?

Once he dropped his lips to hers, her hands laced behind his neck, bringing him closer. The closeness and electric sensations touched her toes, causing her to rise on her tiptoes. Neither of them fumbled, both needing permission to experience a kiss again.

He pulled away first, allowing Amy to breathe. "Just one?"

She giggled. "For now. That one needs to settle." Her lips pulsated with the newness, stimulated by his touch. At the moment, she didn't care about the unknown lurking in the rational part of her. For now, the tangible won the prominent place—a place free of fear and taboo.

He let her breathing return to normal, curtailing all temptations with his distancing. Posing with his arms crossed and back to the opposite counter, he grinned a bit too wide. If someone saw him, the person would know he had done something forbidden. Well, it wasn't forbidden if she gave her permission. Anyway, who would really care what they did?

Don't forget Joshua, Megan, and Lucy. And possibly his employer. What will Maki say if I shared it with her? Things were a lot simpler a few months ago.

"Let's go for a walk," Walker suggested. "I promise to keep my distance, except for holding your hand."

As if that would calm her heart to a normal beat. What was his heartbeat telling him?

Slow down, Amy. A kiss and handholding do not a catastrophe make.

15

*W*alker had lost control of reality. If last night was any indication of things to come, he had some high-stepping to do for everything to fall in place. He'd let enough time pass to rid his mind of the mystic island spell. Being with Amy, even in domestic chores, woke his senses from a two-year slumber.

Concentrate. What do I think I'm doing? I still have time to redirect or pull out of this island oasis.

Pray.

Hadn't he done that already? Surely, God directed him in this bizarre path. Otherwise, Walker would never have veered so far from his set ways. Perhaps, Megan's ferocious reprimands had merit. But if this desire flowed from God's purpose, all involved better take heed, especially Walker.

He grabbed a piece of paper from his desk and set to work on his to-do list, a normal chore, yet with abnormal scribbling this time. His professor friends and daughters might ridicule his list: 1) school play and projects 2) contact the University of New Mexico for a potential job transfer 3) Thanksgiving kitchen duties 4) contact Jean Girard about island cruise.

He almost added: call Megan and Lucy and test their moods. Nope, not today. There was no place for their high alert naysaying, especially Megan's. Her words would sting for a while.

Securing his list with a volcanic rock, he ran his fingers through his unruly hair that matched his two-day stubble. He kept going back and forth—to shave or not to shave. Amy said she liked his island look. Whatever that meant, because he had seen everything out here—long and short hair, beard and no beard, scruffy and clean-shaven.

Stepping onto the long veranda, facing the rugged interior and lush lawn with swaying palms and forest vegetation, Walker searched for Amy, who dominated his waking hours—and his dreams, if he were honest. She whipped in and out of the kitchen in a red bandana print skirt. Her red short-sleeved peasant blouse flowed with the breeze. He'd prefer a kiss this morning, though breakfast would have to suffice instead. The other guests would give Amy no peace if he repeated last night's encounter.

But I will at some point.

Walker sat with the British couple, who regaled him with their recent adventure to Brazil. They knew how to throw off the robes of wealth and mingle with the local societies. The Amazon always fascinated him.

As Amy set out trays of fruit, eggs, meats, and pastries, Walker secured his plate and casually joined her at the side bar. "I believe I have a healthy appetite this morning."

She elbowed him and winked. "More than usual?"

"I think so." He noticed her hands disappear in her pockets. Probably a good thing. Less for him to touch, accidentally or purposefully.

Scooting to the side, Amy avoided his stare. He didn't want the distance or the awkward moments. After arranging already perfect platters, Amy faced him, her smile and sparkle in place. "Will you have time this afternoon to meet with all the teachers to brainstorm about the Christmas play and projects?"

He added something new to his plate, wrapped in thick, green banana plant leaves. The card read eggs and sweet rice. "Already on my list. If you need me this morning, I'll be on the beach, staring into the electric-blue depths." Goofy and poetic. What was happening to him? "I'll either be dozing or reading. I have some details to iron out for the university." He closed the distance, and whispered, "Join me, if you have time."

No response. Was that good or bad? A nod would have eased his worries. Shrugging shoulders boded against him. Dismissed, he strode back to his seat and the Amazon saga.

Flirting, kissing, winking. What was she doing? Rule number one—no romantic relationship with a guest. It had worked for years. Why now? At first Walker seemed as harmless as hundreds of others. She placed her hands in the warm water, hoping the mundane task of soaking a pan would loosen a bit of her crazy notions.

Oh, the kiss. How she tried to bury it in dreams, but it sprang to life at daybreak. Busyness in the kitchen proved a false consolation, for Walker would, of course, show up for breakfast. And then, if she read his eyes correctly, he desired to kiss her again.

No, no, no. He's leaving. His girls will hate me. I will lose my safe existence, depending only on God and myself. No.

But what if God designed this specifically for her? Shivers, reminiscent of cool Oregon nights, shot from head to toe. *I'll listen, Lord, but please let Your hints be loud enough for me to hear.*

She needed reinforcement from her girlfriends. It was about time for a shopping trip. Surely, they would help her settle and ground her girlish dreams. She'd had young love, been a wife, and become a mother. This new thing was not her, not something she asked to happen.

After phone calls to Beth and Lisette, Amy inspected the clean and dried dishes before retrieving her clipboard from the sturdy easel by the refrigerator.

Thanksgiving dinner. An open invitation to all B & B guests, staff, and local friends had become a Maison Cachée tradition. Amy combined the traditional American fare like turkey, dressing, and sweet potato casserole with South Pacific and local recipes. She pulled her recipe binder from the shelf and added the recipes she had marked with sticky notes to her list. Eggplant in coconut cream, Polynesian macaroni salad, fish tacos, grilled chicken *huli huli*, and Suamalian spare ribs. She quickly added guava cake and Tahitian fruit pudding.

Something for everyone. If someone didn't like turkey then fish was an option. Vegetarian, then the abundance of fruit and vegetables met the needs. What would Walker like? Everything so far. Did people in New Mexico eat the same for Thanksgiving as in Oregon? Should she ask? His appetite hadn't faltered or surprised her, except when he was always willing to try new things.

Giggling at her overcautious critique of her list, she noted her lack of concern about the British and European guests. They could care less about the annual celebration. She counted a total of five Americans available for the feast.

Hearing singing in the hallway, Amy called for her friend. "Maki, would you come approve this menu?"

The bright-eyed woman in a yellow wraparound sarape sashayed into the kitchen, using her dust rag as a dancing partner. "Ah, the Thanksgiving feast. What have you added for this year? You have spoiled my Luke all these years."

Amy tilted her head, used to Luke's compliments, and handed over the clip board. "Make sure I haven't missed anything."

A quick critique garnered Maki's grin and laughter. What could be so funny about food? "I see you are out to impress a certain special guest. Three fish dishes, two chicken ones, and four desserts, plus pecan and pumpkin pie. I'm glad we're able to harvest much of this." Maki's cocked head and crinkled brow lacked words but landed a hard punch.

"Oh, well, I thought..." *What did I think?* "I thought the menu needed some new recipes. You know, for the minister, Luke, and well, the guests too."

"The *guest*, you mean." Maki jerked her head back twice, indicating someone or something beyond Amy's comprehension.

"I don't know what you are talking about."

Harrumph and a snort. "Monsieur Walker. That's who."

What does she know? Did she see our kiss? Surely not. Perhaps I should invite her to join my girls' day out. But no, with that grin, Maki seems more of a matchmaker than someone who would talk some sense into my silly brain. I can't have that.

"He is a guest, and you know my rule."

"A fine rule until you need to break it." Maki traded her rag for a glass of water. "You might be able to hide your feelings from everyone else, even yourself. But not me. Remember, I've been here since the beginning. You, *ma fille*, are falling in love."

Amy rested her chin in her palms with elbows on the kitchen island. Her bottom lip protruded in a pout. "But I can't." No way. Being in love was for the young. But her parents were still in love as were Maki and Luke. The difference was *when* they fell in love. Joshua could fall in love. She, as his mother, could not fall in love.

Quirked eyebrows formed a question mark. "Can't? Who told you that? And you better not put the blame on God. Not the God I know."

Amy lowered her eyelids, blocking out her familiar surroundings and her friend's criticism. More like concern and love for Amy instead of criticism. "Novels. It's always a young heroine who falls in love. Not a middle-aged one. Anyway, I said that I can't because I need to guard my heart. I never want to feel such loss again."

"Oh, *ma chère*. Love for any length of time is worth the possibility of pain. Where is the peace you have claimed for a dozen years?" Maki's brown, sun-kissed hands reached across the counter for Amy's. "Peace, I leave with you. My peace I give to you."

Amy brought one of Maki's hands to her heart. "The peace is here. I just need to be reminded. Thank you."

"And you know what else is there? Enough love to share with someone for the rest of your life. Though, whatever your decision, remember you are never alone. God has you covered."

Walker preferred Amy's company to his own solitary one, even though his outdoor office on the tourist-free beach proved conducive for his wayward thoughts. Or maybe it caused his bizarre wanderings. With the turquoise sea lapping close to his cloth-covered beach lounger, he daydreamed more than planned. Daydreamed of sharing his designs and plans of archeologist progress at Amy's backdoor. But her two-foot shuffle earlier warned him to move slowly. Should he talk to someone? Perhaps Jacques or Luke or the minister? Why involve anybody else when Amy might not have any interest? *A nice—perfect—kiss doesn't make for a blissful future, although that is something missing from my life.*

So, no more kissing or handholding. Not until I get a sign from God along with a go-ahead from a friend and Amy.

Shaking his head with unfamiliar hair brushing his neck, Walker propped his notebook on his raised knees. Down to business. It was up to him to convince the university and the

Suamalie government to grant permission to excavate and educate. All the pieces needed to fall into place.

He drew a village, or a *pā* as the Māori called it, from his study of the Duprée site. Amy's historic village was much smaller. Hers might be more of a family site than a tribe. He drew the outer circle of defense probably from wooden stakes, with a few storehouses and lookout huts. Within the next circle of the *pā*, he added individual homes with wooden frames draped with reeds, palm leaves, or bark. A common kitchen and storehouse completed the village. The place of worship might be on higher ground or a cave.

The words for his proposal sailed across the pages. Not a very good salesman in general, Walker relied on his instincts. He certainly proved a lot better at his job than personal relationships—at least with his daughters and Amy. Was he building the walls or was that God's way of stopping his advancement?

After storing his notebook in a beach hut, Walker strolled the dazzling sands, letting his toes explore the warmth and caress of tiny seashells. His footsteps landed him at Belle Vue café. He ordered a mango smoothie minus the coconut and faced the choppy sea to the north. Amy's beach boasted a calm breaker foam unlike the wild Pacific crests.

The laughter of children playing in the waves focused Walker on the sea of people—all nationalities, sizes, colors, backgrounds. A needed reminder of the God-given ability to co-exist in peace and harmony. If his girls could see his work with the island children, would they accept his choices—whatever they turned out to be?

"Standish?"

Walker turned to his left and waved. "Jean, how good to see you."

Jean Girard held the hand of a little girl with the distinct eyes of an islander but with light brown hair bouncing with curls.

"Who is this?"

Jean placed a hand on the child's head and beamed his response. "My daughter, Suzette. Meet Dr. Standish."

"My pleasure." Walker extended his hand which she accepted with confidence. She was the age of some of the after-school children, eight, he thought Jean had said before.

"Since I don't have any customers today, we decided to spend the day in town."

The child pulled on Jean's shirt and pointed. *"Puis-je jouer avec mes amis là-bas?"*

Jean pinpointed a group of children by the water's edge. *"Oui, ma petite. Reste près d'ici."*

As she ran to her friends, images of Megan and Lucy on a beach vacation emerged. Such joy in watching them enjoy life. Rebecca had held the girls' hands. *Rebecca.* Two years was as long as a lifetime.

Walker motioned for Jean to join him at one of the tables. "Would you like one of these delectable drinks?"

Jean nodded as he caught a server's attention. *"Un* coconut ice, *s'il vous plaît."*

Walker liked this young man. He had his own successful business and had time for his daughter. "You have a very special little girl."

Eyes glued to the ocean's edge, Jean puckered his lips and half-smiled. "Yes, as you know, she's all I have. I don't think I mentioned what happened to my wife after she left us." He paused. "She died a few years ago from a heart disease."

Yes, Jean and Suzette were alone, not unlike Walker, just a different age. "I'm sorry. All of it must have been very difficult."

"Yes, but one great thing about the island culture is how the people stop in and help. I have literally had a village help rear my daughter. I'm really sorry Suzette's mother never found true happiness."

Walker conjured up an image of Amy with her *village,*

looking after her son. From all he heard and knew, Amy survived and thrived because of this culture and its love of life.

Jean sipped his drink while watching Suzette every second. "I got your message about booking a day cruise of the islands. Any more details?"

Walker's Christmas cruise idea for Amy rattled his brain at night. Would she want to spend a whole day with him on a boat, stopping to explore a few islands? Should it be a surprise? He'd have to give her some hint in order for her to be absent from the Maison Cachée.

Leaning forward and lacing his fingers together, Walker tried to appear confident, but as he stared at confidence and loyalty in Jean's young, eager countenance, Walker faltered. "You might entertain this as silly for an old man." He paused and after detecting neither impatience nor laughter, he continued. "I want to surprise Mrs. Lee with a day away from the B & B."

Jean smiled, still no chuckles or ridicule. Perhaps it was a better idea than Walker thought. "She will love it. I have some ideas, if you don't. We'll make it memorable."

A strong current of air escaped Walker's lungs. Nerves? Anticipation? It was only Amy, a friend. More than a friend. But how much more?

16

*J*acques Duprée's phone call and subsequent visit couldn't have come at a better time. How it happened exactly when Walker needed the boost had to be a God thing. Could be Jacques fit one of the puzzle pieces in a personal and professional sense. How much Walker would divulge about Amy, he hadn't figured out. But he was a wide-open book about his archeological endeavors.

The Duprée Plantation green Jeep, with the top up for sun protection and the dampness of the jungle, arrived on time. Nine in the morning was normal for Walker. But that meant an early departure from the Duprée Plantation.

Walker rose from his seat at the breakfast table, catching Amy's wave and perky smile upon seeing her friends. Her orange blouse reminded him of a tropical sunset. The color probably had an artsy name. The white skirt emphasized her tan legs. He almost forgot his reason for leaving the table. It wasn't originally just to gawk at Amy. Since her destination mimicked his, he followed her. Close enough to grab her hand, he decided against it. He had to talk to Jacques first. Maybe. It depended on how the morning progressed. Could he claim Jacques as a friend, a confidant, after one meeting?

Lisette handed her big basket to her husband before hugging Amy and spinning them around as school girls. Were the women starved for time together? Amy had Maki and Nadine. Sisterly companionship. Shared memories and experiences. Years. Something he didn't have with anyone else here. Something he wanted, but it rested out of his grasp.

Jacques extended his free hand to Walker. "Nice of you to allow me to spend the day with you. I needed a break, and Lisette doesn't like driving through the jungle by herself. We're waiting for that interstate to come through." He laughed.

Walker assured him the prospect of company settled well with him. "You might regret it after I pick your brain about your plantation and dig site."

The man threw his head back and let out a loud guffaw. "Finally, someone who understands me. We have uninterrupted hours to outline our plans while the girls shop and talk." Jacques leaned in for a whisper. "I'd hate to be privy to all they will share today."

Walker would love to know. Would Amy mention him? Do women still share such details as a first kiss? Lisette was a long-time married woman. Beth? He had no idea. Surely, they wouldn't be all giggly and silly. After all, the kiss was serious and possibly appropriate. Right?

After depositing the basket on the kitchen counter, Jacques retrieved his personal bag. Sort of like a briefcase but bigger. "The good stuff. I've brought some of my paperwork for the dig site on the plantation."

"If all of that is governmental papers, it's worse than the U.S."

"No, it's not so much. Lots of pictures. Like a scrapbook. These are all copies, of course."

Walker itched to get his hands on the papers. At home they'd all be under lock and key and labeled "Out of Public Viewing," even the copies. They'd have to be checked out by signing on the dotted line.

"What's in the basket?" Walker lifted his head toward the kitchen.

"Lunch. Lisette didn't want us to starve."

"No chance of that happening with a café close by."

"I told her that, but you know women. They think we are helpless at times."

Did Walker know women and the way they think? Not anymore. He did want to know one woman and what she thought about certain things.

Amy and Lisette met them in the foyer, purses and sunglasses ready. Walker felt a little out of place with the good-byes. He stood to the side as the couple exchanged cheek kisses. Amy nodded at Walker. She'd left Maki in charge, not him, so no last-minute reminders. His goal surrounded keeping Jacques entertained. No problem at all.

Amy waved to them. "We'll be home around five o'clock."

Awkwardly, Walker lifted his hand. "Have fun."

Jacques added a jovial, "Don't spend all our money."

Amy turned the Jeep around in the drive and slowly left the premises.

The men set up camp in the barn on a big work table, leaving the surfaces and rooms in the house free for the guests. Pictures and maps covered the area in no time. Walker's papers for Amy's project wouldn't take up so much space. Not yet. At least, not with the one cave. If other remnants of dwellings popped up, it would be a longer project. He hoped so.

"Jacques, what do you think the ladies talk about for hours?"

"Oh, I don't know. Us?"

"Well, you for sure. Not me."

The man grabbed a chair and straddled it backwards. His *tsk tsk* didn't bode well for Walker. "You don't think these women are talking about you? Let me tell you. Lisette brings you up in conversation every day, always linked with Amy's name. 'Walker, this. Walker, that.' Where do you think she gets her information, hmm?"

Amy mentions him to her friend? "Is it good or bad stuff?"

Jacques spread out some numbered pictures, forming a timeline. "Do you really want to know?"

"Well…yes. I hope I'm not making a bad impression."

"All good, my friend. Let me ask you a question. What do you think about Amy?"

Basketball court talk. "She's great." Not too much information.

"That's it. So, how do you feel about this great woman?"

Feel? Jacques fished for information he hadn't put into words yet. "Feel? So out of my league here. If I start having feelings for Amy, I'm in trouble."

"Start? I think you already do."

"Well…I…how do you know that?"

Jacques rested his chin on the back of the chair. "I watched you at our house, and I'm listening to you now. Your eyes roam and follow her movements. And remember, you began this conversation. I've known Amy a long time. She's never talked about anyone else like this. Not since Neil."

Walker paced, then stared at the ceiling. "What do I do? I have a life thousands of miles away. I have two daughters who think I'm crazy. I have a job that I love. And this…" His arms stretched, encompassing the room and beyond. "This is paradise and not real."

"If this is paradise, it sure is hard work. Anyway, people fall in love in paradise. It becomes home like any other place. The difference is with whom you share it."

Walker shook his head, trying to solve the puzzle from pottery shards. "I don't think she feels the same."

Jacques jumped up, knocking the chair over. "Ha. I knew it.

You've fallen for her. I promise you, from what Amy's shared with Lisette, she has it bad for you."

Really? Now what do I do with an answer like that? Too much information. "Let's leave my love life alone and concentrate on what you've brought to show me. Really, the tangible proof is more to my liking."

"Yes, women don't really fall into the realm of concrete and predictable."

Lord, show me. I'm a bit lost with this discovery.

Amy parked her Jeep in a small out of the way parking lot, away from the crowds. At least on Alexandre, the car traffic was minimal since tourists seldom rented cars on the small islands.

Porte d'Or boasted quite a few unique shops as well as the essential ones for the islanders. Doctors, lawyers, hospital workers, mechanics all had offices and businesses in this city. Amy tried to buy locally from Belle Vue and the venders in the market but her shopping bug found appeasement here and in Laumua.

Lisette linked her arm with Amy's. Years ago, Amy resigned herself to her friend's model-like beauty and height. Never would Amy be blonde with flawless, glowing skin, and five-foot-eight. Lisette didn't care, so neither did she.

"Where to first, Amy?"

"We have an hour before we meet Beth. Let's knock out the boring must-haves first. So, the hardware store, the feed store, and the pharmacy."

The feed store doubled as a pet store. Lisette picked up hamster and turtle food while Amy stocked up on some fancy cat food and cat treats.

"Your girls still have their hamsters, I see."

"Two became ten. You don't want one, do you?"

"No, but this store might take some off your hands."

"They should. We supposedly bought two males."

"Oops."

Lisette picked up a can of the cat food. "What does Walker think of your cats?"

"What?" Why was that important? "I have no idea. I assume he likes Theo. I've found him petting him in his lap."

"Well, that's good." Her friend replaced the can and batted her eyes.

What wasn't she saying? Asking would open a discussion Amy planned on saving for lunch when she hoped for two allies. She might have just one if Lisette's comment was any indication.

Mouth closed. I will not add to her speculations.

Prescriptions, nails, screws, and light bulbs. They still had plenty of room in the Jeep. Hands and arms free again, Amy anticipated the camaraderie over the next few hours. "Plenty of time to grab a table at Café d'Or."

On the outside the restaurant resembled a petit café. But the hidden jewel opened onto a terrace with a tropical jungle theme. The vegetation reminded Amy of her gardens. Anyone could get the island experience with the waterfalls, ponds, flowers, and native birds right here in a small haven in the city.

A few minutes after they settled, Beth swept her miniature form in canary yellow across the patio. "There you are" rang for all to hear. Amy, Lisette, and Beth hugged and giggled before forming a more mature group at their table.

Ah, mes amies. I need them. These bursts of unrehearsed joy rejuvenate me. Bring it on, girlfriends.

Beth never lacked for conversation. Amy wondered at her energy. "Tell me everything, Lisette, about your girls and David. Oh, and don't forget Jacques. Such a nice-looking man."

Lisette beamed. "Of course, and I want to catch up about your girls and Tom."

Amy's friends knew about Joshua since she'd seen them both separately and spoken on the phone with Lisette often. What she didn't expect was the sabotage by both women at the same time as if planned. They stared her down, and one of them, or both, said, "And tell us all about Dr. Walker."

How did the questions turn to her before they got a word out about their own families? This was not going as planned. Not at all.

"Walker?" Truth or a fib? "He's an awesome guest."

The women, one blonde, one brunette, one short, one tall, mimicked each other with elbows on the table and unblinking stare downs.

Beth led the brigade. "Okay, about *Monsieur* Awesome."

Scream? Run? Hide? Or face the calvary?

"All right, but I want to order first. I need fortification."

Beth motioned the server over in a second. Within five minutes, fruity drinks arrived and gave Amy something to do with her hands and a way to pause the conversation. "Now that you have your nourishment, tell us all." Beth laced her fingers around the cold glass.

After a big gulp, Amy hoped she was doing the right thing and not stirring up a tropical storm. She knew ahead of time that her unfaithful eyes would deceive her anyway. Part of her wanted to shout, while another to whisper. Either way, the truth seemed best. If she could find the truth.

"So, Walker is…a friend. An awesome friend. But 'awesome' means many things. First you need to know, I'm not searching for romance or a fling or a husband." They nodded. Of course, they knew that after all the men they'd sent her way. "I'm shocked and confused why after all these years, one man has made such an impression."

"How? Tell me more." Lisette winked. Amy wouldn't be surprised if her friend broke out in song, as in the lyrics "Was it love at first sight?" from the *Grease* song "Tell Me More."

Her heavy sigh wouldn't make her confession easier, but it did give her clear lungs. "I find Walker's presence invigorating. I want to be with him, sharing in his day. He's courteous, helpful, attentive, funny, and very smart—way more intelligent than I am."

Lisette raised her frosted glass. "And handsome—that never hurts."

Amy smiled, as two lorikeets sang to each other in a nearby lavender bush. "Yes, there is that."

This time Beth sighed, leaning into her palm. "Sounds like you've found someone to share your days and possibly your future."

Amy's staccato answer punctuated the air. "Not. At. All. Those dreamy eyes and intelligence come with a four-thousand-mile distance, two protective daughters, and a fulfilling job. There's no room for me. Anyway, there was only one kiss."

Glasses pounded the table and jaws dropped. Oops, she'd forgotten that little detail. Trouble brewed with the omission.

"A kiss?" in unison forced Amy's continued confession.

"Well, yes. Our one and only kiss, although there's been lots of handholding."

Beth and Lisette grabbed each other's hands and beamed in solidarity, eyes popping at the news. Beth put into words probably what Lisette thought. "And what are you doing about this? Are you planning a second kiss? Or a wedding maybe?"

Amy caught herself before spraying mango smoothie across the table. Swallowing quickly, Amy chastised her friends, and herself, for having these thoughts. "No. No, I can't. We...well... we mentioned having a second kiss, but it never happened. He knows as well as I do that this...whatever this is...cannot work. We're friends. That's all. Now, I've told you everything. We can move on to talking about anything else but me, or more specifically, Walker and me." The end. Although she didn't want it to be the end. But with no solution, it had to be.

Beth dug into her salad, talking between bites. "Did you hear about the wedding planners on Cadeau Île called 'Something Suamalie'? I'm dying for someone to use them. Then there's the photographer, Haley."

Amy might as well have laughed. Pushing her plate aside, she smacked her lips and waved her hands, crossing them in front of her face. "Enough. There will be no wedding, so save your brain cells."

The two sets of wide eyes studied her. Lisette shrugged her shoulders. "Well, we'll just have to save our talent for someone who appreciates us. Maybe Nadine will get the wedding bug. Or David or Joshua?"

Their laughter garnered a few stares from neighboring tables. "I know I don't want Joshua getting married anytime soon. How about we talk about something else. My love life, or lack of, has run its course."

Beth stole the check from the end of the table. "My treat."

Amy and Lisette rolled their eyes, and Amy beat Lisette to the usual response: "I'll get dessert later."

"Thank you, ladies," Lisette bowed in acknowledgement, "I accept your generosity. Now, *allons-y*. Shopping awaits."

Leaving the bills on the table, Beth grabbed her purse. "I want to check out a new boutique and see if the owner wants to sell my soaps and lotions. I have a bag of samples. Always."

Once outside the café, Amy squeezed between her friends, linking arms, pulling them close. "Thank you. No matter what happens, I do feel better for airing out my almost love life."

They managed yellow-brick-road steps with a myriad of pleasant subjects to buoy their afternoon.

Amy wondered how Walker and Jacques had spent their hours. Hopefully, not on the same subject.

17

A week later Amy and Maki put the finishing touches on the tables decorated with straw turkeys, gourds, orange and gold fat candles, and plenty of fabric fall leaves. Island fall was different than the ones in Oregon. Here the greens and yellows and reds remained bright and full of life. The decorations served as a reminder of her first home, a part of her but not her whole.

"*Parfait*, Maki. *Merci beaucoup*. Now, for the rolls and the guests."

Maki clapped her hands in approval and readiness. "I hear some guests already. The smell of the turkey and all the spices must have drawn them. Cinnamon and cloves do it every time."

As Amy rescued the last yeast rolls from the oven, Walker entered the kitchen, dressed in his khakis and a button dress shirt. She giggled, no island attire for this American feast. She had on a simple dark-green knit dress, the closest she could get to a fall color. "I was wondering when you'd show up."

Walker draped his arm across her shoulders and kissed the top of her head. "Happy Thanksgiving. You are making a lot of people happy."

She drizzled butter over the rolls. "Even though half of them have no idea what Thanksgiving is."

"Exactly. They know it is special to you, so they participate with glee."

"Well, Mr. Happy, help me carry these last plates to the dining room."

"Yes, ma'am."

Amy studied the faces of those gathered around the tables. Guests, friends, family, and Walker. He occupied his own category. Each day he felt more like family than friend. Family was permanent, even if miles separated them. Could he even be closer than family? There had been no repeat of their kiss. She'd made sure to keep her distance or her defenses would crumble, leaving an unsightly mess when he left. Her friends helped her see her folly, at least in her eyes. They still thought things could work out with Walker. Amy guessed married people assumed everyone should be married.

Walker's hand on her arm pulled her back to the task. Whispering for her benefit, he said, "I think they are waiting for you to say something."

She nodded, stood, and addressed the guests—her family for the day. "Welcome to this Thanksgiving table. It is the custom in the States to gather with friends and family and give thanks for God's rich blessings. Well, you are my family and my friends. Pastor Logan, will you offer a blessing for this food?"

Heads around the table bowed in thanksgiving and praise. Some held hands. Amy offered her own thanks in her heart for each soul here, and for Joshua, apart from her this Thanksgiving.

Walker sat next to her at the large family table. His hand covered hers a few times as conversation flowed. This event confirmed once again that Maison Cachée continued to bless and offer solace and reprieve from life's stress. No magic took away the problems, but a peace soothed the edges and put things in perspective. She couldn't promise that for everyone, but she believed it possible.

The colorful assortment of fish and veggies disappeared with the turkey and dressing. American and South Pacifica united in fellowship.

Thank you, Lord.

"Do you think I could persuade you to walk on the beach with me? With everyone napping this afternoon, it might be just the two of us."

Just the two of us. I've avoided that for a while, hoping my infatuation might dwindle. Nope. I don't see that happening. A walk, holding hands, the ocean. All will work against what I've thought appropriate.

Amy sighed. "I think that is exactly what I need. I never want to eat again. I should have passed on the pecan pie."

Chuckling, he secured her hand in his and led her toward the path to the shore. The palm and banana leaves reached for them as well as the hibiscus and orange trumpet.

As the scenery changed from flowering jungle to iridescent sea, Walker stopped—he always did. "I can see why you stayed, Amy. This paradise has quickly captured my heart." He glanced at her, finding her openmouthed and teary. What did he say to cause her reaction?

She swallowed, then whispered, "Enough to stay?"

He willed his shoulder to remain still. A shrug would leave too much doubt. "It is an option. But I have a few months to see what happens."

"Yes, two months."

Their hands remained laced. He made sure she couldn't pull away. Swinging their arms, they strolled in silence, pausing as two porpoises played in the distance.

"I have a surprise for you. An early Christmas present." She pulled against his hand and opened her mouth again. He put a finger on her lips. "I cleared your calendar for Tuesday. Maki and Nadine have everything under control, even breakfast for your guests."

"But..."

"Amy, I want to spend the entire day with you. I've rented a boat and a guide for the day. We have it all planned. Please say yes."

She bit her bottom lip and squeaked, "Yes?"

"That sounds like a question. I want you to be sure."

She pulled her shoulders back as if the task had a level of extreme seriousness. "Yes, I would love to go with you."

He embraced her and spun her around. The beach, the ocean, and Amy. "That is a relief. I've lost a bit of sleep over this. I wondered if you'd rather a helicopter ride with Flora Bishop?" But that couldn't last all day. Maybe as a second outing.

With her arms around his neck, Amy peered at him through damp lashes. "The cruise is perfect. I look forward to it. Tuesday? Do I need any more details?" She lowered her arms and gained her footing. A hand went to her cheeks, rosier than earlier.

"I've had lots of help. So, everything will be taken care of. I just need you to be ready by eight o'clock. Dress comfortably."

Amy tilted her head and grinned. "I have something for you in the library. Just a small gift, not for Christmas, or any occasion really."

He claimed her stray hand again. "What is it?"

"I had Ezra from the Title Wave..."

"Is that the boat bookstore?"

"Yes, exactly. Well, she dropped off a copy I'd ordered for you of *Sea People* by Christina Thompson."

"I'm so glad. Perfect. I've wanted that for my research."

"I knew you would. I have my own copy in my room. It explains a lot about the South Pacific islands."

As twilight worked its magic, splashing colors across the waves, Walker turned Amy towards him. Just one more kiss. "I think I want that second kiss now."

Amy's eyelashes fluttered, but she didn't pull away. "I think that would be the perfect ending for today."

And every day?

The warmth of their kiss held promises of more. This was the greatest blessing of this Thanksgiving Day. At least for him.

18

For the tenth time, Amy put another outfit on her bed. Shorts? Skirt? Sarong? Pants? She placed her hands on her cheeks, warm and clammy, whether from concern or anticipation.

Would their second kiss lead to a third or fourth? She'd not shared any more information with Lisette and Beth. Not yet. The day in front of her might answer a few questions or leave her with many more. What was the point? Another opportunity to close a few gaps, though four thousand miles proved a large chasm.

"What am I to wear on this...date?" The walls couldn't tell her. If she asked Nadine or Maki, then they'd know of her fear and nerves. And would they have any better answers? Probably more like Beth and Lisette encouraging her to follow love and take a risk. "A date on a boat for hours with Walker, as a man, not a guest. Am I crazy?"

Hands on hips, she had to make a decision. "Okay. Not a skirt or a dress." She held a pair of royal blue capris next to a short-sleeved blouse with small blue dots dispersed all over it. The oversized shirt would allow for cooling air and easy movement. If she knew exactly where Walker was taking her, the choice might be easier. Or not? Even one date lurked outside her comfort zone.

She dropped her hiking shoes and socks in her bag, just in case. A hat, sunglasses, bathing suit...

Within a few minutes, Amy appeared dressed for an island adventure—one she had not planned, not even one detail. The role reversal added an element of excitement. If only she could relax into that position. She hadn't relinquished control in a long time.

Twirling in front of the mirror, Amy decided primping anymore wouldn't change a thing. "Let's do this."

With her light load, Amy accepted the carefree parameter Walker provided for today alone. It's not as if he offered to plan her life. One day. No expectations of her, and she set aside any for Walker. Free to see what a different view could open up for her. *It's in Your hands, Lord.*

Swinging her hat in one hand, Amy almost skipped down the pier but decided to save that for another time. No reason to scare Walker away with her childish exuberance. Her gait slowed when she saw Walker poised as a sentinel beside the cruiser. Breathtaking in navy cargo pants and a white polo with a denim, three-quarters sleeve jacket. Crisp, casual, and sophisticated at the same time. Handsome with a quirky grin. What hid behind his sunshades?

Help me not fall for his charm any more than I already have.

"Captain Standish, I presume."

He laughed and extended his hand for her steps onto the boat. "Perhaps, skipper or deck hand. I'll leave the captain label for Jean."

Her hand in his warmed her in the cool morning breeze. A whole day of his attention could prove dangerous for her heart. "Wise decision, skipper."

"Anyway, you are my only focus for the next twelve hours or so."

"That is a long time to spend with me. Are you sure you're up to it?" *Am I?* The warmth of his presence with the island sun as a constant might be a tad more than she could take.

Pushing his sunglasses onto his head, his eyes reflected the sparkling water. "Oh, *ma chère.* I'm more than ready. You?"

Finding her footing on the slightly rocking boat, Amy joined the banter. "Well, I think if I can survive a boat full of guests, I can handle one man."

That sounded a bit flirty, but why not? This is a date, a Christmas gift with the man I have kissed more than once. But flirting had never been her forte, even as a teenager or young adult.

Amy found Jean as he finished the preparations. "Thank you for being available. How much planning did you two do?"

"A lot. I'm excited about this day also. Rarely do I get to take only two people on a cruise. I must say I enjoyed the planning with Walker. I want you to sit back and enjoy the ride."

She sat by Walker on a long bench awaiting Jean's instructions. "There are plenty of drinks in the refrigerator and snacks, although I think Walker has an abundance of items to satisfy any culinary cravings. Relax and have fun. Our first stop is in a little over half an hour on the isle of St. Alyn. I'll let Walker fill in the details." Jean saluted and gained his post at the wheel in the enclosed cabin, giving Amy and Walker a shield of audible privacy.

Sit back. Relax. I can do this.

Walker handed her a tall, cool orange concoction. "I had Maki mix up a refreshing morning drink—mandarin and mango."

Her fingers touched his as she accepted the glass. "Cheers, Walker. Thank you for this excursion."

He sat next to her on the starboard side of the boat for the best view of the islands. One of his arms draped the rail behind the cushioned bench. Very close to her. She could easily transition into his close embrace.

"I hope you are pleasantly impressed with my planning skills."

She still knew nothing of the details, and surprisingly, she liked it this way. "Anything at all will be amazing. It's a gift enough not being in charge."

"So, you still trust me with the details? We haven't even made it to the first island."

"How many islands are we visiting?" What surprises awaited her? She'd been to all the islands many times. Anything was possible. Knowing Walker, he'd done his research.

"Counting Alexandre, five."

So far, so good. Walker drummed his fingers on the rail, waiting for contact with Amy's shoulder. Time. Not in the first ten minutes. He had all day.

Her brown wavy hair played in the breeze. The water lacked the swells of late morning when many boats created the bumpy waves. The slow speed glided the boat across the turquoise-tinted sea. Jean had been correct about the pristine surface in the early hours. What would he have done without his input? Probably started with a turbulent ride.

"I know you've been to all the islands and experienced far more than I have. Our first stop is a catered breakfast in a beach hut on St. Alyn."

Amy smacked her lips. "Perfect. I don't know of any restaurant there that offers breakfast except at the hotels."

"Ah. I pulled some strings. The Blue Fish is supplying the meal."

"*Bien.* The chef is a personal friend."

"So, that is why he was so willing. I thought it was my persuasive skills."

The long pier suspended on the sea led them to a thatched hut with strings of lights, some piped-in local music, flowers, and a table full of the island's best selection of food.

Amy sat on the sofa-bench beside Walker, claiming the best view for both of them as the ocean awoke with activity—fowl, mammal, and motors. He had Amy and delectable nourishment. What more could he want at the moment? Since he didn't have to think beyond that, his answer was nothing. He had it all.

He lifted his cup of rich, island-blend coffee to his lips. "I still wonder at the freshness of the island food. I know I couldn't go in my backyard in New Mexico and come back with a meal of any kind."

Amy plopped a mango slice in her mouth and offered him one. "I know. Oregon isn't known for tropical fruits either. Now, if I want a really good steak, the beef doesn't compare to Texas or the Southwest."

They shared a laugh or two about what they missed about the States. He noticed Amy's list was very short. Glancing from Amy to the water to the rich vegetation, Walker realized he could live on the islands, Alexandre in particular, for the rest of his life. But the picture included Amy. What would she think of his business proposal?

Walker decided against resting his arm too close to Amy. "I have some news about all the paperwork I submitted."

She turned, facing him. "Oh, I hope it is news you want."

I want? What if she doesn't want it? "What if I say it depends on you?"

Her jaw dropped as her hand fluttered to her chest, and she batted her eyelashes. "*Moi. Je ne comprends pas.* Surely, I can't help very much."

He chuckled and leaned forward, letting their knees touch. If he secured her hands in his, would it be easier? No, he had all day to make his move.

"I'll need a place to stay for another six months while I search for a house to rent. Do you think you could stand me for half a year more?"

Her "yes" glistened in the morning light. Tears? Or the sun? "Oh, Walker. I'm so happy for you. Of course, you can reside at Maison Cachée for as long as you want. No one has booked your suite yet. I also have plans to renovate two cabins into complete studio apartments. Maybe that would do."

He read her grin and shaky voice as permission to lace his fingers with hers. "You won't tire of me?"

Leaning forward until her forehead touched his, Amy whispered, "Not of you. You do realize the B & B is closed during February, so the amenities will be few."

He squeezed her hand and sighed. "I think I will actually like it better that way."

The moment ended with a server's arrival with boxes for the leftovers. "I'll take these to the boat for you."

"*Merci.*" Walker stood, bringing Amy to her feet. "As much as I want to stay, we have our next appointment on Tiga."

Crinkling her brow, Amy's big expressive eyes relayed curiosity. "Not even a hint?"

He shook his head, grabbed her hand, and left their little piece of paradise with boxes of goodies tied with strings. This spot, no more idyllic in natural beauty than other island views, would cement a place in his memory because of Amy.

Jean deposited them on Tiga where they followed a path spilling over with hibiscus, lavender jacaranda bushes, and fruit trees. "If it's more food, I don't think I can eat a thing." Amy rubbed her belly.

"No, you will have to work for your next meal."

"Oh?" The path opened into a grassy knoll with a hut containing several rooms open to the outside. "I've not been here before." She thought she'd been to most every place on the islands. How did Walker find this place?

"That's because it's a new set-up. A traveling classroom."

Amy shaded her eyes with her hand. "Is that Sabrina Wheeler? What's she...?"

Before she could finish, the colorfully dressed woman stepped from the veranda. "Amy, *talofa*! I've anticipated this visit." Sabrina winked at Walker.

Amy crossed her arms, eyeing both of them with suspicion. "What have you done?" *We're in the middle of a field with a talented artist, winking at my...well, at Walker.*

Walker raised his hands in defeat or guilt. "I had help."

Amy clasped her hands and steepled them under her chin, never taking her eyes off of the guilty party. "I'm sure you did."

Sabrina grasped Amy's hand, leading her up the steps to a large open room. "*Bienvenue* to my pottery classroom."

Giggling with girlish glee, Amy twirled around, noting the table covered with supplies. Though she'd never made anything out of mud or clay before, she recognized the tools.

Walker stood by Sabrina smiling—very pleased with himself. "I think she is surprised."

Sabrina resumed command. Amy surrendered to the student role, eager to learn. More amazed at Walker's gift than the actual class, Amy stared at him and mouthed, "*Merci*."

Amy sat down and motioned for Walker to do the same. "You are participating, right? If not, I'm going to make it a requirement."

He nodded and plopped down opposite her. "I wasn't going to miss this chance to get muddy. Anyway, it's nice to know how to create some of the things I dig up so often. Maybe someone will find my pottery shards in a thousand years."

Sabrina passed out aprons and tied her bright red one around her. *"Bien, mes étudiants,* a bowl, a cup, or a vase for your first attempt? I expect you to take another class later where you can attempt something else."

"Vase." Amy rubbed her hands together. Her own creation for her flowers. Would it even hold water?

"Cup. Maybe for the B & B's famous smoothies."

Working across from Walker gave Amy a sense of domestic tranquility. Their goals in the task were different—hers aesthetic, his practical. How would their lives mesh—if things progressed—into a routine? She knew she would support his archeological quests, and he'd already shown he wouldn't mind sharing in the running of the B & B. She hadn't considered a partner in such a long time. Why was she thinking about it now while molding a simple—very simple—vase?

Amy presented her vase with a very long neck for inspection. "Do you think this will go with my decor? Or should I put it on a shelf in my closet for Joshua to find years from now?"

Holding his lopsided cup on his palm, Walker grinned. "I'll put mine with yours. I do know no one can find a match for it."

Sabrina praised their work, just as Amy did with her art students. "Your first attempts are wonderful. Next time, we'll work on form. This lesson got you used to the feel of the clay and the wheel. I'll expect you to continue your pottery lessons when you can."

Amy glanced at Sabrina's creation—a perfectly symmetrical bowl that would definitely hold water and serve as stylish decor. "Will I ever be able to make something like that? I think I need to stick to my canvas."

"Let me take your masterpieces." Sabrina set them in a safe place on another table. "I'll fire and glaze them for you. You might be surprised at how imperfections in the raw change with a bit of attention and polish."

Walker stood and removed his apron. "Do you think mine

will hold liquid?"

"I do. Hot or cold. Thank you for trying something new."

"It gives me an appreciation for the pottery that I find. It amazes me when a whole vessel is recovered intact."

Amy studied their creations with a different interest. What people leave behind told a lot about what they valued. Yet, she'd heard that many facts about ancient people were found in what they discarded. That made her want to cherish her misshapen vase all the more.

After washing her hands in the basin, Amy checked her clothes and skin for any remnants of clay. All clear. "Thank you, Sabrina, for the lesson. I'll be in soon to purchase some Christmas gifts."

"Ah, don't remind me. I still have so many orders to fill in the next few weeks."

Amy bent in for a hug. "That should be a good problem."

"Yes, you are right. Why complain, when I love what I do? Be safe and have fun on the rest of your cruise."

Walker shared a nod and a quirky smile with Sabrina as he guided Amy down the steps. It appeared everyone knew about her "date" and destinations except for herself. So far, it was wonderful and clever.

Amy glanced behind her and waved. "*Tofa*, Sabrina. I think we'll work out how to add pottery lessons to our school program."

As Amy and Walker approached the cruiser, Jean set his reading material aside. He must benefit from the Tidal Wave's services, too, especially with a young daughter.

"Success, *monsieur*?" Jean's grin matched Walker's. *They sure are a proud pair.*

"I can't speak for the lady, but yes for me."

"And me too. How two men thought of something so unique is inspiring."

Amy chose a seat in the sun, hoping her hat and sunscreen

would shield her from any harmful rays. A boat ride on the turquoise water with a brilliant sun and ocean breeze clamored toward perfection.

Walker left a whisper of a centimeter between them as he draped his arm around her, rocking her towards him. Perfection eased closer, if her heart could handle the interference.

"Next stop, the Mercer Plantation on Olioli for an afternoon repast."

Consulting her stomach and hunger meter, Amy admitted her appetite had returned. "Onward, then. If only the islands were further apart." She really didn't mean to add the last part. But it was true.

Walker laughed, not letting the comment slip by. "Why, Amy?"

Her belly knotted from frustration as she elbowed him. "You probably know why." Pausing before commenting more allowed her words to form from her thoughts. Sometimes she used her filter but maybe not enough. "Because I'd rather have more time with you just like this." There. Out there for exploration.

"Hmmm. Or this?" He guided her chin toward his and kissed her gently before sealing it with a deeper bond.

His eyes, darkened by the sun but more likely by passion, asked her questions she couldn't answer. Not right now. Not today. And maybe not ever.

"Yes, or that." Glancing around, Amy focused on the back of Jean's head. "You must trust him."

"I do. But remember, you've done nothing to merit any gossip."

"Haven't I? A widow for twelve years kissing in broad daylight might be fuel for gossip."

Her fingers rested on her lips. *Have I done anything worthy of scrutiny? If Maki or Nadine knew of any rumors, they would come straight to me. No gossip, just facts. The facts scare me more than any gossip.*

19

The Mercer Plantation catered to the tourist desiring an off-the-beaten-path experience. Jean had toured the place many times and eaten there a half-dozen. He promised it would never be overly crowded. Anyway, they were hitting it at a mid-afternoon hour. In the States, that would guarantee fewer people, but Walker had noticed islanders didn't necessarily stick to rigid schedules.

"I thought we might need the steps, so I've mapped out the path to the back of the plantation. There is an entrance and a beautiful avenue of trees and gardens. Are you up to a little trek?"

"By all means. It's hard to get the needed exercise on a boat."

"I don't think you'll need your hiking shoes, so you can unload them here."

"How did you know I had those? I really didn't know what to bring."

Walker helped Jean secure the boat at the pier. "When I moved the bag earlier, it was heavy, and I saw the source."

She discarded the shoes and grabbed the lighter bag. "*Allons-y, mon ami.* I'm ready to see another place I've never been and to eat. How did you manage to find someplace else I hadn't been?"

"Maybe, I spoke to a few of your friends. Mainly Maki. So far, has it been okay?"

She stepped onto the pier and offered him a hand. "More like perfect."

He didn't need her help, but he made sure he kept her hand in his. The journey led them from the beach directly onto the property, through a manicured jungle, if there was such a thing, through lawns bordered by native plants, fountains, statues—a bit European—mini-orchards, until they reached a large covered patio with tables and umbrellas, and only one other couple.

Walker guided her to a small podium at the base of some steps. "It seems like we almost have the place to ourselves."

A gray-haired, dark-skinned man greeted them. "*Bienvenues. Vous êtes* Dr. Standish, *n'est-ce pas?*"

"*Oui, nous avons une réservation pour deux.*"

"*Je suis Monsieur Mercer. Suivez-moi.*"

The table faced the gardens with the water features gurgling and the birds singing in the background. Walker could not have chosen better music. Amy beamed her appreciation of the beauty. This hidden jewel should be in every guidebook but he understood why it wasn't. How would it appear overrun with tourists?

"Are you the owner of the plantation, Monsieur Mercer?" Amy asked the question that had turned around in Walker's head.

"*Oui, Madame.* I enjoy meeting the patrons. I take a shift every once in a while."

Amy nodded. "I understand entirely. I run a B & B on Alexandre. I love meeting the guests, eating with them, and showing them the islands."

"Ah, I've heard of you. The young owner of the Maison

Cachée. I've heard great things. Perhaps my wife and I will escape to Alexandre sometime soon."

Blushing, Amy accepted the menu and the compliment. "You will be welcome anytime." She glanced at the assortment of dishes. "Since I can't have one of everything, what do you suggest for appetizer and entrée?"

He pointed out a few suggestions. In mere seconds, they had ordered vanilla-seared scallops and crab rangoon for appetizers, and caramelized pork chops and banana leaf chicken with pineapple, fried rice, and jack fruit curry for their entrees. The idea was to share everything. Walker wouldn't mind doing that for the rest of his life.

Amy set her glass of mango tea on the table and patted her lips with her napkin. Her flushed cheeks and glistening eyes pulled him forward. "Walker, this place, this day, has been so special. I don't really understand all my feelings and thoughts. Is there any way you could help me?"

Help her? When I don't know anything either? It appears this day has sparked the conversation I desire.

He put his palms up on the table, inviting her to reach out to him. She did. "Amy, I don't have the answers we need. I do know that I don't want this to end. I want to see where this relationship will go. I have no desire to leave you, Alexandre, or all that life here involves. There are a few obstacles though."

He bowed his head in concern. When he joined his gaze with hers again, they both said in unison, "Our children."

Amy squeezed his fingers and bit her bottom lip. "Don't we have the right to make our own decisions? I've not said anything to Joshua. I'd want him to understand, but I'm scared he won't." She scrunched her nose while tilting her head.

"I understand. If I said anything to Megan and Lucy, they'd have me committed. But I think Megan guesses something is different."

Placing one hand on top of his, Amy patted him. He could

feel her concerns beating through her fingers. Could they do this together? "I have to live my own life, not my children's. I'm the parent, not the child."

She giggled. "I feel like a teenager though. I've had one love. Do I deserve another? Shouldn't I be content with being a mother and maybe a grandmother?"

"Did I hear you say 'love'? Do you possibly love me?" His words didn't sound like his own. Love? Could she?

"Maybe...I don't know. Even a budding romance is out of the question."

"Why, because we are older? Because we've loved before? Because of our children? If we eliminated those obstacles, would you consider loving me?"

Laughter surrounded them. That was the last thing he anticipated for a response. She brought his hand to her cheek. "Silly man, those don't stop me from loving you. Nothing will stop that. They might deter the advancement of this...this courtship, but not the love."

"That's a relief." He chuckled. "I thought I was going to have to abandon my children and act and look younger. Ah, Amy, I love you. I want to try to make this work, whatever this is."

"Well, this is a fine Christmas gift. I love you too."

He kissed her fingers, saving a proper kiss for the walk to the boat. Or better yet, for the last part of their journey. Love? The admission startled him, not the fact that he loved her. But that she loved him—that hit him hard.

After the fabulous meal with fresh plantation produce and their over-the-top admission of mutual emotions and love, Walker chose the west side of Lafoina for a spectacular sunset. A blanket, fruit, sparkling cider, and Amy, a woman he loved.

As he stroked her fingers and fell under the spell of the

orange, red, and yellow masterpiece unfolding over the ocean, his heart skipped a few beats. Love? Could it be real? And she felt it too?

A mature love, not a young adult love triggered by relentless hormones and overzealous plans. He'd have to ponder this new realm of attraction, admiration, and adoration. He had the time now that words had been spoken, releasing things they had danced around for a while.

And he had her heart, as well as her hand.

Lifting her long fingers to his lips, he added a volume of questions and feelings with few words. Her clear eyes, mirroring the sunset and his own image, gazed at him, expecting something. What, he couldn't pinpoint. A kiss for sure. "Amy, I want more days and evenings like this with you. On your beach or any others, at your house, really anywhere. Will you give me a chance to share in your paradise?"

A few tears coursed down her cheek, and she nodded. "Yes. Whatever that looks like. We have time to figure it out."

"I want to share something I memorized from Psalms before I left for the islands. 'If I ride the wings of the morning, if I dwell by the farthest oceans, even there Your hand will guide me, and Your strength will support me.'" Walker glanced at Amy, never tiring of her expressions. "If this is part of God's plan, the pieces will fall in place. It might not be in our timing, but it will happen."

The drama of the sunset, and a rather long, impressive kiss, sealed their revelation of love.

20

a week later, the sweet revelation of their love, exposed on a romantic cruise with a man Amy could truly love, seemed foreign and make-believe. She fluffed pillows and straightened bed covers for the hundredth time. So much concern over Joshua. Why? A few months ago, she didn't know if she could live without him. Could her heart be so weak as to allow someone else close? Close enough to scoot her longing for her son's return to the peripheral? Was it one or the other?

Nope. The problem rested in her choice. A choice to keep Walker a secret. Not one word. Joshua arrived today for Christmas break, and Amy had locked her feelings for Walker in a safe department. Except for Maki and Luke. Every time Walker mentioned the children, Amy froze. She wanted the secret unexposed for a little longer.

Well, the box was about to spring open. Joshua would know, somehow. Anyway, Amy doubted she could bottle up her emotions and screw the lid on tight.

Tap. Tap "Are you ready?" Walker filled the doorway to a guest's sitting room, with his arms crossed and his partial grin in place. He had a bunch to risk too. If for some reason Joshua disapproved, Amy would have serious choices to make.

"That's a loaded question. You don't have to go with me." *But I do want your strength. Why didn't I tell Joshua?*

"I'll be right by your side in whatever role you want."

As she turned off the light, Walker bent and kissed her. "That might be the last one for a while."

The trudge to the pier pounded with her sporadic heartbeat. *Please, Lord, give Joshua an open heart or...or what? Okay. I'm giving this to You.* Again.

Walker squeezed her hand as the boat approached, then he stepped back. In a few minutes and a few miles away, Amy saw Joshua at the railing, waving just like he had as a child and youth. Amy lifted her hand in an exuberant rainbow wave from side to side.

It is going to be just fine. My boy is home.

Fine, until Walker exclaimed, or grunted, "Oh, no!"

Amy jerked her hand down to her side in time to see his face crumble from assurance to surprise to shock. Where was her rock? "What?"

He pointed a shaky finger to the boat. "See that woman next to the guy I assume is Joshua?"

"Yes, I don't know her though."

He spurted out between gritted teeth. "I. Do. That is Megan, my daughter."

Amy covered her mouth, preventing a shout or a snort or a huge burst of laughter. "Oh, no, is right."

As the cruiser inched closer, the pair on board stood in drastic contrast. Joshua, smiling and energetic. Megan, scowling and rigid.

Walker's heavy sigh released his woe and added to hers. "I promise. I didn't know." She believed him and felt his anguish.

How Amy wanted his hand, or his arm around her, or his kiss. But that would send Megan overboard, for sure.

Amy laughed instead. *God sure has a sense of humor.*

"We can do this, Walker. There is plenty of room for love."

Sharing a wink and a smile, they faced their children together.

The End

AUTHOR'S NOTE

I appreciate the opportunity to be a part of this amazing series. I loved (am loving) the research on the South Pacific and applying it to the fictional Suamalie Islands. Always a student of languages, culture, and history, I try to find those interesting tidbits to add to my writing—food, travel, language, native and natural history. I've spent time on Maui and remember the mesmerizing features and beauty of island life. My bucket list includes Bora Bora!

The foreign languages I use in these stories are French and Samoan. I hope the reader appreciates the cultural experience in these French Protectorate islands along with native culture—a true hybrid existence. Amy's B & B, the archeological digs, and the plantations fulfill my love of history. I hope you will continue with the series and gain a new home among the islands.

BIBLIOGRAPHY

Charles Rivers Editors. *Mysterious Polynesia*. Charles Rivers Editors, 2021.

Higham, Charles. *The Maoris*. Cambridge: Cambridge University Press, 1983.

Rawlings-Way, Charles, Brett Atkinson, Jean-Bernard Carillet, Paul Harding, Craig

McLachlan, and Tamara Sheward. *Lonely Planet South Pacific*. Lonely Planet Global Limited, 2016.

Spencer, Sarah. *Totally Polynesian: Classic Recipes from Polynesia*. Create Space, 2017.

Stevens, J. R. *Polynesian Cuisine*. Encore Publications, 2017.

Thompson, Christina. *Sea People*. London: William Collins, 2020.

ABOUT THE AUTHOR

Marguerite enjoys the study of history, especially when combined with fiction. An avid traveler and reader, she teaches French and Spanish and has degrees in French, Spanish, and Journalism from Trinity University in San Antonio, Texas and a MA in English from Hardin-Simmons University in Abilene. She has two grown children and currently lives with her husband in north Louisiana. She writes historical fiction.

facebook.com/Marguerite-Martin-Gray-261131773910522

instagram.com/margueritemgray

bookbub.com/authors/marguerite-martin-gray

goodreads.com/margueritemartingray

amazon.com/author/margueritemartingray

ALSO BY MARGUERITE MARTIN GRAY

AN UNEXPECTED GIFT

SUAMALIE ISLANDS YEAR ONE BOOK SEVEN SNEAK PEEK

MELISSA WARDWELL

1

_K_iana groaned inside as her dragon lady boss, Anita, continued the public reprimand, yelling loud enough for all of Le Cadeau Île to hear. The bride who stood before her on the pedestal froze in terror, her mouth agape as Anita slammed something on the counter. Kiana could feel the tension rise as the bride's entourage murmured amongst themselves.

"Is she always like this?" The bride asked.

She couldn't honestly answer the question due to being contractually bound to be silent in all things said and heard within the salon. Kiana met the bride's gaze through the mirror after fluffing the train of the gown she had been admiring.

"You look stunning, Lauren. I don't know how you will decide," she said with a stiff smile.

Lauren gave her knowing look and nodded her head in agreement. "It is definitely difficult to decide between this and the Oscar de la Renta."

"I think you should go with the Alexander McQueen," Lauren's mother announced, unfazed by the drama happening in the receiving area. After three glasses of champagne, the woman was very much relaxed. Kiana learned years ago never to contradict a customer who has sampled the salons perks.

"My hips looked as big as a house in that dress, mother." Lauren's eyes met Kiana's, "but the puff sleeves of this one balances out my voluptuous bottom half. Isn't that right?" She had never had a customer that caught on in such a short amount of time.

"This one does accentuate you in the right ways. But ultimately the decision is yours."

Stepping to the side, Kiana kept one ear trained on the party she was working with while the other ear listened for more of Anita's outbursts. When she was in one of her moods, you never knew who would be next. If her guess was correct, Anita had just hung up the phone on one of their suppliers. She hoped it wasn't one of their top sellers.

Brides came from all around the world to their salon just because they had the most exclusive selection available in Bridal haute couture. If Anita ruined it all because of her sour temper, it would have more than just a lasting effect on the salon but also the resort in which it was housed.

The Grand Paradis Resort was one of the top resort destinations in the world, catering to those who had an unlimited bank account and spent it like it would never run out. Everything was of the best quality and best design. Rosa Aurora Marble Floors and crisp white walls with a marble fountain of the Polynesian god of the ocean, Tangaroa, welcoming each guest. In the guest suites, linen wallpaper adorned with light gray images decorated the walls while Macassar Ebony floors left guests feeling like they were walking on gold.

However, the *pièce de resistance* was the bridal salon and event planning boutique. The same elegance of the resort's lobby was reflected in the on-site business but accented with crystal chandeliers, blush pink velvet couches, and plush white rugs. There were five locations for brides to admire the gowns they tried on under specialized lighting and four walls of mirrors. The gowns ranged from fifteen hundred dollars to twenty thousand dollars, and they were never in shortage of brides looking at the high-end gowns. Like the client Kiana was helping now.

"What do you think, Lauren?" Kiana asked as the bride pet the delicate lace. "Can you see yourself walking down an aisle flanked with various island lilies as your groom waits for you under the arbor?"

Lauren stopped her unconscious petting of the gown, a tell-tale sign that she was about to purchase the dress, as her bottom lip began to quiver. Though tears developed in her eyes, a smile brightened her face. This moment always touched a special place in Kiana's heart because it meant the woman in the gown felt like a work of art.

There was also a part of her that longed for a moment like that for herself. She stopped hoping for it when her thirtieth birthday came a little over a month ago and she had no one to share it with but her friends and coworkers, Lulu and Meilani.

"Yes!" Lauren proclaimed with a squeal all too familiar to Kiana's ears. The bride's entourage surrounded her, sans her mother, giggling and jumping up and down in unison.

Kiana glanced at the mother of the bride and was met with puckered lips and squinted eyes. She had seen this kind of mother before. More than she would've liked. The mother was all about looking the part. They are just committed to a ten-thousand-dollar gown, her mother wanted one that was at least five thousand dollars more. It was status that brought them to the salon, even if the bride was innocent in her mother's game.

Meilani came over at Kiana's signal with all the necessary paperwork to finalize the sale.

"Watch the mother. She's working on her fourth glass of champagne now." Kiana nodded in the woman's direction, whispering in Meilani's ear. Turning to the bridal party, she informed them that her coworker would be taking over, and it was a pleasure working with them. Wishing the bride all the best, and internally praying that her mother didn't continue to use her as a status symbol, Kiana made her way to the break room.

How much longer, Lord? How much longer must I work in such a place? You know I love my job--the brides, the planning, and some of the mothers. It's the greed that gets to me, Lord.

Kiana grabbed her metal water bottle from her designated cubby and flopped unladylike in an uncomfortable pink velvet chair. She closed her eyes, taking several cleansing breaths before taking a drink from her bottle.

"The bride was that bad?" Lulu asked while she sketched the set-up for a wedding for the weekend. One of many.

"No. Lauren was actually a dream to work with." If only her mother saw it. "It was a draining party. I feel like I could sleep for a week right now."

"I think I feel the same. The sketch is never good enough for this bride. Her wedding is in three days and no matter how many times I tell her that this won't be the final outcome, it's just a rendering, she insists that I precisely draw the way it will look. I won't know that until I start putting the fabric on the arbor."

"Lulu, there are just some people you could never make happy."

"And we are in the industry that shows the worst in people."

Lulu's statement reminded Kiana of Anita's outburst. "What was the deal with Anita?"

"Check bounced, again."

A bride from Idaho was to have her wedding in three weeks but her payments kept getting denied. "Anita must've finally gotten a hold of her. There's only so many times you can avoid a phone call from her."

Meilani entered the room, checking her watch for the time

even though there was a large clock on the wall to indicate the hour. "Can we go home yet? I had to practically carry that mother out to the lobby. And the way she talked to me...it was like I was a second-class citizen to her."

"Some of these people seem to take for granted the talents of Suamalie's people while we struggle to have a simple backyard wedding." Lulu lamented with a huff.

Kiana pondered as the conversation continued, taking another swig from her water bottle.

There has to be another way.

Like someone flicking the light switch, a plan formulated. Images of the three of them sitting around a table with a bride and her groom, planning the day of their dreams, danced in her head. The difference was they weren't at the upper-class, sterile salon they worked at now. They were sitting in their own space with their own Suamalie Islands style. The more time she let it brew within her, the more she liked the idea. If only she could get Lulu and Meilani on board.

"Ladies, I have an idea..."

Made in the USA
Monee, IL
01 August 2023

40226985R10113